Brrm! Brrm!

Brrm! Brrm!

or
The Man from Japan
or
Perfume at Anchorage

A NOVEL BY

CLIVE JAMES

JONATHAN CAPE LONDON

First published 1991
© Clive James 1991
Jonathan Cape, 20 Vauxhall Bridge Road, London SW1V 2SA

Clive James has asserted his right
under the Copyright, Designs and Patents Act, 1988
to be identified as the author of this work

A CIP catalogue record for this book
is available from the British Library

ISBN 0-224-03226-7

Typeset by Falcon Graphic Art Ltd
Wallington, Surrey
Printed in Great Britain by
Mackays of Chatham PLC, Chatham, Kent

to Noriko Izumi
for her gift to me, Japan

あなたのおかげです

all other girls grow dull as painted flowers
or flutter harmlessly like coloured flies
whose wings are tangled in the net of leaves
spread by thin boughs that grow behind your eyes.

— Edgell Rickword

Reduce this lady unto marble quickly,
Ray her beauty on a glassy plate,
Rhyme her youth as fast as the granite,
Take her where she trembles, and do not wait,
For now in funeral white they lead her
And crown her queen of the House of No Love:
A dirge, then, for her beauty, Musicians!

— John Crowe Ransom

ONE

B EFORE THE ENGLISH GIRL exploded into his life like
the torch of a flame-thrower through the slit of a pill-box,
Suzuki had been leading the dream existence of every young
Japanese man in London. When dealing with the natives it was
tiresome to feign pleasure at clumsy jokes about how his name
was the same as that of a motor-cycle. But it would have been
impolite not to, and anyway, he did not have to give his name
very often. If he had been working for a big company he would
have had to sit down on the other side of the table from the
local people and Exchange Views, which would have meant an
exchange of names. The same name as the motor-cycle: Oh yes,
most amusing. *Brrm! Brrm!* Ha ha. The famous English sense
of humour, in Suzuki's experience, consisted largely of asking
you to share their delight at a mortal insult. No doubt he was
missing the nuances.

But Suzuki did not work for a big company. He was the
assistant manager of the other Japanese bookshop: not the big,
general one in St Paul's Yard, the small, more specialised one
on the other side of the Cathedral, towards the river. English
people came in there to flick through the art books, ask how

much they cost and retire shocked. Customers were ready to find Japanese books on Japanese art expensive. They were nonplussed to find that Japanese books on European art were expensive too.

'Sixty-five *pounds*? For a book on a French impressionist? That's twice as much as it would cost in France, for Heaven's sake.'

'Sixty-five pounds, yes. I am very sorry.'

'Sixty-five *pounds*? Are you sure you haven't made a mistake with the *yen* or something?'

'The book must come from Japan. It is very expensive.'

'It certainly is. I mean the reproductions are lovely or I wouldn't even be asking. But that's a ridiculous amount of money.'

'Yes.'

'And the text isn't even in English.'

'No.'

Such exchanges sold few books but they were good for Suzuki's English, which he was always very keen to practise. The bookshop was the ideal training ground. It even worked both ways. There was the occasional English language student who was learning Japanese. 'Good day,' he would say, 'the weather is good.' This when it was raining outside so hard that the side of St Paul's looked like a chalk cliff lashed by a typhoon. 'Yes,' Suzuki would say, 'or perhaps the weather is only so-so.' They were always delighted to hear the word for so-so. *Mama*. English modern language students did not know many words so there was rarely an exchange of names. He was safe from jokes about motor-cycles.

Most of the customers were Japanese, including many

pretty girls. Two of the girls who worked with him behind the counter were quite pretty also. Despite his shyness, Suzuki had made friends with them. But he did not unbutton much. One of the girls, Keiko, was married, and the other, Mitsuko, was too advanced. She openly disapproved of the subordinate position of women in Japanese life. Lately she had said that she did not want to go back to Osaka. Suzuki was interested in what she said but did not want to get involved with her while she said it. Though he was going to be a writer, the kind of writing he wanted to do was traditional. While at Tokyo University he had published some short stories in a prominent magazine and on the strength of this auspicious début he had been pleasingly identified as one who wished to restore the limpid values of Kawabata. Suzuki had not thought of it precisely that way before. The minute he heard it said, he decided that it had always been true. Certainly, when he looked back to the famous split between Kawabata and Riichi, Suzuki was on the side of that old delicacy and poise recalling the courtly tradition of the Heian era. He found the School of the New Sensibility aesthetically offensive.

The argument was old by now. Suzuki took sides in it because it involved his temperament. He wanted to see the world, yet he wanted, in his writing, a world reduced to order. Modern life was chaotic even at home. Here, in this foreign land, it was an inferno of unpredictability. Suzuki believed that it was not enough for his work to reflect reality. How can a hand-mirror reflect the lightning? The world must be absorbed, controlled, brought to book. Suzuki knew he had the right cast of mind for this task. He had been tremendous at school, but then young Japanese people always are. More remarkably, he had not wasted his time at university. Japanese universities, even the best ones – face it, even the greatest one, his, Tōdai – are mostly just a beery hiatus between working too hard at school and working too hard at one's career. Suzuki had made sure that he worked too hard at university as well.

Especially he had worked too hard at his spoken English. He had gone at it like a fanatic. While his fellow students were up in Ueno Park getting drunk at blossom parties, he hung around the President Hotel in Aoyama cadging part-time jobs as an interpreter for English and Australian television companies. Written English had always been his best subject. Before he finished school he could read the whole of *The Forsyte Saga*. He soon discovered, after his first contact with outsiders, that there was a world of difference between literature and speech. The same difference obtained, of course, in his own language. He should have realised. It had been a big shock to find out that although he could read all the major works of Galsworthy in the original he could not say the author's name in a way that an English, American or Australian person could understand.

It was small comfort that no American or Australian, and very few people from the United Kingdom, had ever heard of Galsworthy in the first place. He knew that the foreigners were not great readers like his own people. But it had been a humiliation to say 'Galsworthy' and have the name not recognised because the 'l' sound was insufficiently liquid. And, of course, the 'th' sound too sibilant. An Australian television producer, a woman with blotches on her skin that she called freckles, had taught him some good exercises. 'Look, love, let's live a little.' That one had been most useful. 'Colloquialisms too lavishly employed, lad.' That one had been a nightmare, but she had patiently made him say it a million times. 'Thick thews, thin thighs, and thoroughly thoughtless.' Eventually he had learned to say it without needing to mop up afterwards with a Kleenex.

Also she had invited him into her bed, a courtesy which had induced in Suzuki a profound sense of well-being, because of the size of her room. It was the smallest room the President Hotel offered but it was still twice the size of his room at home. And it was in the centre of Tokyo, whereas the apartment his family lived in was more than an hour out of Shinjuku station on the Saitama line. Going to bed with a foreign girl in a huge room in Aoyama made him feel as adventurous as Mishima. Suzuki did not admire Mishima's work: except, of course, for the great *Confessions of a Mask*. But he admired Mishima. Suzuki wanted to be great. Mishima had known how to be a famous man. Unfortunately his notion of fame had entailed early death. Suzuki was definitely not interested in that. Suzuki's literary sensibility was allied with a business brain. His life in London was harmonised in all its facets, his departures from convention being the most thoughtfully calculated elements of all. In the bookshop he was a marked man, as well he might be. Though he deferred properly to the manager, who had seniority, nobody doubted that Suzuki was a meteor on his way through to glory. Not only was he a graduate of Tōdai who had precociously made his name as a writer of promise, but, even more impressive, he had already been chosen for the express elevator to the top level in the governmental bureaucracy which runs Japan.

At some time in the future Suzuki would be a representative in a special new department of cultural relations.

That was why he had been sent to London – to acquire the cosmopolitan ease which cannot be learned at home even in the best schools of etiquette. Suzuki objectively regarded himself as ideal casting for this quasi-diplomatic role. With equal dispassion he knew that his retiring personality was a potential drawback. If he followed his instincts, he would keep his contacts with foreigners to a minimum. At work he could hover behind the counter and say little. At home, his English home, he could lock himself in and say nothing. Home was a bed-sitting room, prodigiously large by Japanese standards, in a back street off Belsize Park Road. Apart from the one evening a week in which he dutifully attended a major cultural event, Suzuki could, and frequently did, sit in his room watching videos, reading his favourite semi-pornographic serials in *Big Comic*, listening to Western classical music on his Boodo-Kahn DD-100, bringing his filing system of culturally interesting press clippings up to date, or practising calligraphy. His one evening per month of hard drinking with acquaintances among Japanese men of his age group should have been enough to take him out of himself. But Suzuki had identified his own shyness, recognised it for a threat, and taken steps to defeat it.

At considerable expense he had joined a health club whose facilities – gymnasium, swimming-pool, squash courts, aerobic dance studios and much else – were built into the preserved shell of an old banking establishment in the city's financial centre, confusingly called the City. At the price of having to endure many a joke about motor-cycles, Suzuki, while volunteering to further harden his already muscular body, was usefully forced to exercise his colloquial English. Not long after he joined, he met a middle-aged English journalist who had reached a very elementary stage of conversational Japanese and wished to go further, into the areas, fraught with difficulty for all outsiders, of actually reading and writing the Japanese language. In the burning white fog of the steam room, the journalist made it clear that he himself would not be returning to the gymnasium, which had done nothing for him except sprain his back.

'The biggest mistake I ever made was coming here, believe me.'

'Yes.'

'I mean, if I was twenty years younger and had a body like yours there'd be some point.'

'Thank you.'

'But I wouldn't submit myself to this again even if they threw you in as my personal trainer.'

'Threw me in?'

'Included you. What else do you do, apart from this nonsense?'

Suzuki conquered his fear of intimacy and seized the opportunity before it disappeared. They came to an arrangement whereby Suzuki would visit the journalist in his flat for three two-hour sessions a week, one hour of each session to be spent talking advanced English, and the other hour to be spent on the rudiments of written Japanese.

The journalist's flat was in the Barbican development, on the side nearest Smithfield market. Suzuki could walk there easily after work. From his viewpoint the arrangement worked well from the start. The journalist made homosexual advances which Suzuki rejected with a suave tact that he was pleased to

15

achieve in a language not his own. Actually he had no moral objection. He simply found the journalist, as he found most outsiders, physically repellent. The thought of a would-be seducer getting unwashed into the bath, and sitting there in his own scum, made Suzuki's face freeze. But the journalist was not without intelligence. He had a knack for explaining tricky English idioms. He had, however, no special gift for acquiring the two Japanese phonetic alphabets, and it was doubtful if he would be able even to make a start with the character alphabet, but his motivation was good. Suzuki conscientiously set out to match his pupil's stumbling eagerness with the long patience of a teacher. At the end of a two-hour session, the journalist, whose name was Rochester, would have learned the difference between, say, 'o' and 'a' in the cursive phonetic script. Suzuki would have learned how a saying like 'I've got him to thank for that' can mean two entirely opposite things without even a difference of emphasis.

Suzuki got the sense that Rochester-*san*'s career on a famous national Sunday newspaper was not going well. 'I'm one step ahead of the boot' was an elegant expression once decoded, but how confusing initially! Suzuki and Rochester-*san* were of one accord. Japanese was insanely difficult to read, and English was insanely difficult to speak. They would shake their heads ruefully at one another, but as Suzuki went roaring home on the incredibly dirty tube train, he felt wealthier than a man visiting a shrine who dips the provided bamboo cup into the drinking fountain and finds himself sipping neat Scotch whisky. He was getting so much the best of the bargain that you could scarcely call it a deal at all. It was more like – what was the phrase? – daylight robbery. Hard to say.

Daylight robbery. Suzuki subvocalised the phrase, but his lips must have moved, because two young English people who were standing up a few feet away started laughing at him. One of them, the girl, had her hair arranged like the spines of a sea cucumber dipped in black lacquer. She wore a brooch of artificial stones in the side of her nose and the clothes of a speedway rider who had been recently buried under a fallen building. The boy had a haircut like the crest on the helmet of a Roman officer, while his skull and face had been painted to recall the helmet itself. He wore a chain-mail shirt, paratroop pants, and a pair of boots that looked as if a baseball had been stuffed into each toe. Suzuki thought with nostalgia of his nights out in Akasaka when he and his fellow high-school students had considered it daring to share a dish of ice-cream in the Western-style *patisserie*. He held his mouth rigid and just thought the words. *Daylight robbery*.

It went almost without saying that Suzuki would have been a catch for any Japanese girl in London. He avoided, however, even the hint of an entanglement. In Tokyo, when there were still a few shot-traps in his carapace, before he had learned the full measure of his present caution, he had been on the point of becoming engaged to a quite unsuitable girl. It had taken the combined efforts of his mother and sister to separate him from the snare. In London he saw Japanese girls occasionally, but only in social groups. For anything more serious he had recourse, as seldom as his healthily urgent needs allowed, to English massage girls who wore nothing under their nurse's uniforms. Their lack of cleanliness sometimes made him gag and even the pretty ones were no pleasure to the eye when one looked closely. In Tokyo he enjoyed going to the kind of bar where you could inspect the genitals of the hostess from close range. Clinical cleanliness was so basic to the transaction that it did not need to be mentioned. To try the same thing with an English prostitute would be like conducting a survey of industrial pollution. As a man who didn't like to run risks, Suzuki was doing his best to contain himself. *Big Comic* helped. *Bon Comic* was even better, being more like hard pornography, but it had to be carefully concealed from the landlady, who might not have survived an encounter with its illustrations, especially the ones in the small advertisements for such harmless devices as double-pronged spiked vibrators with warm water ejaculation reservoirs, clear plastic sphincter-viewing tubes, serrated nipple clips and self-lubricating artificial vaginas. *Big Comic* was reasonably safe. Apart from the occasional full-page illustration of a bound, naked girl shouting with pleasure while being forced to straddle on tip-toe a bar-stool covered with cactus leaves, it was quite decorous.

For some time Suzuki's only relationship with a Western woman had been with the tall blonde American criminal princess in *Big Comic* whose handsome Japanese lover buried his head between her legs while she was on the telephone giving orders to her twin black assassins. Lying naked on his little bed with the comic held open above him, Suzuki in his fantasies imagined himself in the position of the lover. For the short while that each bout of self-satisfaction lasted, he felt cause to regret that his affair with the Australian television producer had so quickly come to an end. He could see now that he had underplayed his hand. He had made himself too available. Instead of commuting home each night at a decent hour he had checked himself in to a capsule hotel, so as to be able to linger with her in her enormous room without having to worry about catching the last train. Having inconvenienced himself to such an extent, he had pressed for favours in recompense, pushing her further and faster than her reserve allowed. He should have kept things so that it was always she who had to ask. He easily could have. Finally she had become frightened, and had restored the status of mere friendship, leaving him to stew with politely masked annoyance. Luckily her camera crew did not know about the affair, so the humiliation was merely wounding, instead of intolerable. What haunted him still, though, was not the embarrassment but the fact that he had miscalculated. Properly managed, the liaison would have lasted until the day she left Japan, and been renewed each time that she came back – as she would have done, because they always come back to Japan. Suzuki had learned from his experience. He never made the same mistake twice. But really he preferred not to make a mistake even once.

To the casual eye, then, the well-placed Suzuki seemed as easily at home as any civilised young man could be in a barbarous foreign city. A more expert gaze would have detected that he was perpetually alert, balanced lightly on the balls of his feet, ready for any impact. It is a characteristic of ambition to expect the unexpected. What is known can be dealt with automatically. There is energy in reserve to deal with the unknown, which, if not precisely welcome, at least poses only a dilemma, rather than threatening paralysis. Suzuki knew that the English girl was unstable the moment he saw her. Three Japanese girl tourists, after browsing for an hour at the magazine racks while dutifully obeying the written injunction not to remove the polythene wrappers from the latest issues of *More*, *With* and *Glossy*, had finally settled for buying one copy of *Jump Comic* to share among them. By the time he had given them their change and they were on their way out of the shop giggling, the English girl had already arrived, penetrated as far as the art book shelves, and begun to treat one of the most expensive boxed books as if she owned it. Her appearance was startling enough. In Tokyo you could see punk young people in the Shibuya district at night, but few of them cared, or dared, to adopt the whole panoply of this most aberrant among Western fashions. Instead they wore tokens. A girl would have a safety-pin through her ear but be wearing a school blazer. A boy would have green hair and big boots, but his leather suit would look tailored. Wildness was strictly controlled. The visual impact of this girl was out of hand from top to bottom. None of it even looked particularly meant. She was not like one of those exotic works of art he had seen on the tube train, or queueing in Soho or Oxford Street to get into an all-night dance hall. Her spiky blonde hair was not a creation. It was an accident. It not only looked dyed, it looked dead. In a ghostly white face her large eyes were black-rimmed: a pistol had been fired twice at point blank range through a sheet of paper. Her mouth, painted crimson, hung open as if she had to breathe through it. The teeth inside it were the neatest thing about her. Neat teeth were important to Suzuki, a member of the new Japanese generation whose dentition is in such good shape that they can afford to be critical of their elders.

Below the head, the girl's body might have been strong and healthy. It was difficult to tell. Though her black T-shirt looked as if it might be covering very large breasts, a baggy black jacket, too heavy for a fine late winter day like this, covered the T-shirt. If the trousers had been baggy also, the ensemble might have looked intentional, like something by a good Japanese designer – Yohji, for example. But she was wearing what looked like the bottom half of a tight black sweat-suit made for someone much smaller. Between the hems of her leggings and the tops of her huge black boots there was a double dose of startling white shin. She would have been disturbing to look at even in repose. She moved constantly, with no clear purpose. Suzuki knew the word for it: fidget. He even knew the phrase: to have some fidgets. No, to have *the* fidgets. This girl had the fidgets. She slapped her way through the double-coated art paper pages of the hugely expensive book. Suzuki could tell which one it was. It was the beautiful book about Japanese industrial design and marketing campaigns. Mostly it consisted of photographs but the captions were in Japanese. The girl had evidently been made impatient by this latter fact. She put the book roughly back in the box without first aligning the wrapper with the book proper. There would be bound to be some creasing caused to the wrapper. She looked impatient while she was doing this, as if it were the fault of the book, or the box, or both. Having accomplished the task to standards which she evidently deemed good enough, she put the book back in the wrong place without even looking, cramming it into the shelf until it made a sufficient space.

Meanwhile she was looking at books about Japan in the shelves which had previously been behind her, but which she was now half facing. Most of these books, like the one she had just been looking at, were written in the Japanese language.

In a Japanese bookshop this should have been no great surprise. Her impatience only increased. Seemingly preferring
the devil she knew, she turned back to the shelves at which
she had just rummaged. Suzuki was fascinated to note that
her turning movement, while in no way simple, could not
be described as complex either. It was merely random. She
travelled in six different directions, settling on one of them
after growing tired of the others. She searched the shelves
with an impatience which made her previous agitation look
like the schooled calm of a tea master. Finally she found what
she had been looking for. It was the same boxed book that
she had previously maltreated. She pulled it roughly from
the shelf as though to punish it for having hidden. Pulling
it from its box looked more difficult than it ought to have
been. Suzuki assumed that this was because the wrapper was
crumpled from the previous attack. He decided it was time to
intervene. Leaving the desk in the care of Keiko and Mitsuko,
he threaded his way between the customers surrounding the
low horizontal display areas of newly published books, headed
down the alley between the high shelves, and held his open
hand just above the girl's forearm.

'Here,' he said. 'Let me show you.'

'About time,' said the girl. 'It's fucking *stuck*.'

'I'm afraid that's because you caused it a certain amount
of damage when you first took it out of the box,' said Suzuki
with the casual triumph of a diver who successfully completes
three and a half forward somersaults from the high tower and
surfaces to find that his entry into the pool has caused scarcely
a ripple. It had been a difficult sentence to bring off, especially
with the 'because' and the 'caused' so close together. But he

had not panicked. He was in command. It was his favourite feeling. Most Japanese men, if they were sworn at in their opening encounter with a Western woman, would behave as if they had been cut off at the knees by a ceremonial sword: a sudden smile and they would fall away. Suzuki forged on.

'I hate having to ask you to be more careful,' he said, 'but the book is very dear.'

'How much is it then?' she said scornfully.

'I meant very precious. But also it is very expensive, yes.'

He told her how much it was. She pronounced the sum ridiculous. With phrases polished by constant use, he explained to her how much it cost to bring books from Japan. The girl announced that in that case she would have to read the book in the shop. She described herself as a free-lance journalist doing an article about Japan. The article was in an advanced stage but she needed a few more facts. Telling him all this took ten times as long as it would have taken any other human being he had ever met, because of the way her speech wandered.

'. . . and they *knew* that if they wanted *me* to do it, they'd *have* to *pay* me, because of all the money they *owed* me, so of course they *panicked*, just the way they did when they owed me money in the *band*. I was a singer you know, still am really, but who wants that? Because you *have* to do what you're the only one, don't I? Who can do it properly, and I'm the *only one* who can do this kind of article, that's been *proved* . . .'

Suzuki let it all pass over him because he did not know how to stop it. There were very few full stops. Eventually there was a question mark that he thought he could respond

23

to. If he was free after work, she suggested or requested, perhaps he would like to help her? Agreeing without hesitation, Suzuki steered her back to the desk and gave her his card. Like most Westerners she did not have a card of her own. He gave her a piece of the bookshop's writing-paper so that she could write down her name and address. She grew impatient with the ball-point pen he lent her, and positively enraged with the paper for not being the right width. Just watching her go out of the door was like being the eye-witness to a car crash. For the two hours left in the working day, Suzuki examined his heart to find out why he had succumbed. The answer seemed inescapable. He craved danger. But he was not the man for that. Perhaps he would have to change himself. He was not the man for that either.

TWO

L UCKILY IT WAS NOT one of his evenings to visit Roch-
ester-*san*. That was an arrangement Suzuki never disturbed if he could help it, although he might have done so
in this case. He was in credit with Rochester-*san*, who often
had to go away at short notice. In credit was the way Suzuki
liked to be. Consulting his *A–Z*, he found that the girl had not
been lying when she said she lived within walking distance.
Her name was near the top of the piece of paper, printed in
that sprawling way which declared that she had not been one
of the lucky few among her compatriots to have been taught
the cursive Italic script at school. Jane Austen. He recognised
it immediately as the name of a great English writer. He had
read *Sense and Sensibility* in the original and had answered the
question about it in one of his examination papers. It must
be difficult for the girl to have the same name, especially in
a country where it was so uncommon for someone to be called
exactly the same thing as someone else. No doubt she had to
endure jokes, as he did. Perhaps that was part of the explanation for her behaviour. Suzuki walked up Aldersgate Street
past the Barbican tube station and turned left at the crossroads.

The address was a high-rise building in a narrow street behind City Road, next to a warehouse full of photographers' studios. There was a scarred metal panel of entryphone buttons. He pressed the designated button and waited to hear her voice. Three quarters of an hour later he was still waiting. Then he heard it behind him.

'Oh, it's *you*,' she said in the dazed manner which he had already recognised as standard. 'Am I late? I had to go out for five minutes to get some things.'

'I was here at the time agreed,' said Suzuki.

'How was *I* to know you'd find the place? Most people can't. Lot of the time *I* can't, as a matter of fact.' While saying this she was trying to get her keys out of her jacket pocket without putting down two plastic carrier bags that clinked heavily. It would have been easier if she had put them down. He offered to carry both the bags, which made it much simpler when they were inside for her to press the call button for the lift. Nevertheless she almost missed the button at the first push. The button was metal, set flush with a metal plate. Suzuki was impressed that her finger was half on the button and half on the plate when she started to push, so that her effort was disproportionate, indeed mainly wasted. The resistance made her impatient. She swore at the lift in terms he found startling, not for their shock value but for the expenditure of effort. Would she have anything left to say about something serious?

When the lift door opened, the lift itself proved also to be made of metal, like the call button and its plate. The all-metal interior of the lift had a rippled surface, perhaps with the intention of frustrating vandals. If so, only a relative success had been attained. Displayed from floor to ceiling on the back wall of the lift, in acrylic black paint from which Suzuki's fingernail was unable to flake a chip, there was an announcement, purportedly emanating from a black man, declaring what he would like to do to a white schoolgirl with his erect virile organ, whose improbable dimensions were supplied. No doubt the intention was racially inflammatory. Like all the graffiti which Suzuki had seen lavished with such insane prodigality on the helpless bare public surfaces of London, this rubric offended him less for its content than for its want of art. In New York a certain level of calligraphic skill had been achieved. During his brief, bewildered visit to that city he had seen subway cars which had delighted him with their intricately worked surfaces. But this effort conveyed nothing except a slovenly urge to self-expression trying to dignify itself as sexual psychosis.

'Oh, yeah,' said the girl, looking back over her shoulder. 'That.' Suzuki was interested in the way she used the one word 'that' to cover a subject that she felt not worth giving one of her usual long speeches about. Her alternative strategy, he soon discovered, was to say nothing at all. When she opened the door to her flat, a profound verbal apology for the appearance of its interior would have been appropriate, although not sufficient. It looked as if it had been ransacked by thieves who had been forced to desist only by the eventual discovery that there was nothing to steal. Although moved to sympathise, Suzuki forbore, construing her silence on the subject as confirmation that she always lived like this. Stretching his powers of detachment to the limit, Suzuki strove to imagine what it would be like to be faced with such disorder and not feel impelled to correct it. His room in Japan came into his mind, with its boxes within boxes stacked on top of the wardrobe: so much material packed into a small area that each disturbance had to be rectified immediately or it would be impossible to get through the door. This girl treated her living area as if it were the space between stars. Clothes littered the floor and the unmade bed. Further trails of discarded apparel led off into the bathroom – he could see a sweater draped over the edge of the bath – and into what looked like a kitchenette. Clearly she got dressed and undressed the way she walked, in a movement constantly modified by unexpected encounters with inanimate objects. Those belongings which were not stacked on the floor were strewn – arranged would have been too strong a word – on olive drab metal shelves which had been built out of some kind of erector set. At least half her books had been inserted into the shelves back to front. There were audio components which might once have formed a stack but were now widely spaced, joined only with wires. The portable television set belonged in a museum. At the moment it was leaning precariously at the foot of the bed. The walls featured a lot of photographs cut out of newspapers and magazines. Enough of the original wallpaper showed through to show why she might have thought it needed covering up. There were many posters, among them several for a pop group whose name he did not recognise. The best poster was in Japanese.

'That's my Japanese poster,' said the girl, managing to wave at it while looking the other way. 'It says something about lotus blossoms mingling with the ashes of the slain heroes or something. You know, something about all those blossoms they have there, and the way they, hey that's *you*, isn't it? *You'd* know. The way they worship the slain heroes with blossoms. That's what it says. Japanese writing. My *friend* told me. He's *lived* there. It says something about the ashes and the blossoms.'

'No,' said Suzuki kindly. 'It says something about the Mitsui Bank's summer art exhibition.'

'See,' said the girl, as if running out of patience with a slow pupil. 'I didn't *know* that. So how am I going to finish this fucking article?'

In the course of the next hour it gradually became clear that she had not started the article. After Suzuki had been given an impossibly large drink from one of the several bottles of vodka the girl took out of the heavier of her two shopping bags, he was ordered to sit down on the bed, whereupon he was supplied with copies of the magazines in which articles by Jane Austen had appeared. Apparently her real name was Jane Osmond, but she had changed it for professional purposes. Before becoming a writer she had been with a pop group, which according to her testimony had been quite famous. With it she had toured the whole world, including Japan. Some of the posters on the wall, she explained, were for that pop group. Her face appeared in only one of them, somewhere at the edge of the band, as if she were part of the décor. He suspected her of leading a marginal existence. As far as he could tell, her articles were written with inside knowledge and some fluency, but the magazines to which they had been contributed were for that part of the youth market where titles like *Face*, *Blitz*, *I.D.* and *Arena* all covered the same few subjects at once. The only difference between those well-known publications and these that featured her articles was that these were skimpier looking and had far fewer advertisements. Since the whole point of such publications was to secure advertising, Suzuki doubted whether his new acquaintance was being paid very well, or at all. When he asked to see the manuscript of her article about Japan, so that he could comment on it, she said that so far it existed only in note form. When he asked to see the notes, they too were not forthcoming. She gave a superfluity of reasons. When the pop group broke up she had never been paid the money she was owed. The magazines paid her as little as they possibly could. It was impossible to concentrate on writing because the bank kept ringing her up about her overdraft. Also there was the constant threat of losing her flat, which belonged to the council. She owed the council some rent, although nothing like as much as the council said. There were people at the council who specialised in victimising young people. They would have her out if they could. Luckily she had a medical certificate. Suzuki asked her what kind of medical certificate it was. She said it was for mental disturbance.

When she was getting off the drugs, she explained, she had attempted suicide once or twice and they had given her a certificate for it, which she was now clinging on to for dear life, although naturally she was full of contempt for the sort of official mind which would hang a tag of mental instability on anything it couldn't understand. Suzuki had already noticed her wrists. With her jacket removed, her body had revealed itself to be built on a substantial scale. He had been right about her breasts. They filled out her T-shirt in an impressive manner. Her wrists, however, were the focus of his eyes. On her white skin, the scars were brown, like faded ink. They reflected her character by going in six different directions. Her speech, too, he now realised, was not just random but violent. Everyone who had ever refused her was a wanker, a bastard or a cunt. Her bank manager was a wanker, a bastard *and* a cunt. Suzuki nodded in agreement while the tirade continued, as if he understood. Actually he was manfully striving to bring his capacity for comprehension into line with this latest, most extreme manifestation of the semantic anarchy in which people condemned to use the English language managed to convey meaning to one another without dying on the spot from shame.

In Japanese the levels of politeness were so precisely codified that one could convey an insult merely by eliding the end of a verb. But the point was that both speaker and listener knew exactly what was going on. All speech was conversation: it was communal or it was nothing. In English you could talk to yourself in the presence of other people, as if their feelings not only did not matter, but did not even exist. Suzuki found this aspect of his voluntary exile the hardest to get used to. Merely listening to people talking in the tube, he took a linguistic battering that frequently left him punch-drunk. In the street, asking someone the way to somewhere, he would receive a reply which left him no honourable alternative except to challenge his interlocutor to a duel. At the gymnasium, when he sat in one of the Nautilus machines and worked to improve a specific group of muscles, he had to field shafts of boisterous familiarity which would have been more appropriate if he were manacled to the wall and in the process of being flayed. But all these linguistic atrocities, though they had happened well-nigh continuously for more than a year, were bagatelles compared with what this girl could unleash in a few sentences. Suzuki felt a sort of relief, as if a long-threatened war had finally broken out. What was the phrase? All bets were on. No: off. All bets were off. It was too late to tell her that 'Suzuki' was the second most common name in Japan. She was too busy calling some editor or other a wanker. When she asked him his first name, he told her without hesitation: Akira. She greeted this intimacy with the same blank look of token curiosity which had been engendered by his family name. He had taken that non-committal glaze of feigned interest as a courtesy, but now realised that she had simply never heard of the motor-cycle. Then, with an abruptness that Suzuki had not yet learned to expect, but which he gathered he had better get used to, the girl changed tack.

'Look,' she said, looking away. 'I have to go out soon.'

'Well,' said Suzuki, so much at a loss that he lapsed into a construction from his own language, 'If I don't go, it will be bad.'

'Well,' said the girl, looking at the Mitsui poster as if addressing it instead of him, 'Don't you want to kiss me?'

Suzuki, who at this point, having quit the bed during her monologue, was sitting on the only chair in the room, almost fell off it, but gathered himself sufficiently to drop gently to his knees and thus bring his face almost level with that of the girl, who was sitting on the bed with her legs to one side, for once having adopted a pose befitting a woman. As carefully as if he was still negotiating his first waltz at ballroom-dancing class, Suzuki kissed her crimson mouth. Like all Western people she smelled of butter. In her case the odour was bearable. Her eyes were shut. His, open, could detect the layer of white paint on her face. He wondered why she troubled to make

32

up her skin. It was so white anyway, except, of course, at the wrists. One of them, the right one, the one she was not supporting herself on, he caressed with his fingertips. When he returned his eyes to hers, they were open but gone. She was looking away into the kitchen, perhaps worried that the bailiffs might arrive through the window. When he tried to kiss her again she shook her head like someone being pestered by a fly. But she agreed to meet him a few days later. Now that he knew the way, he was to call on her. It was no use trying to phone at the moment because there was some mix-up about the bill. Anyway, she had to go to Paris. But by the appointed day she would be back.

THREE

WINTER WAS ALTERING to spring. When Suzuki reached the street it was still twilight. The towers of the Barbican were not yet silhouettes, though their stained grey concrete teeth cut sharply into the pale sky. Feeling buoyant, Suzuki decided against travelling on the Circle line. Instead he walked on down Aldersgate Street towards St Paul's station, with the intention of taking the Central line. He relished every step. The area was full of Japanese office workers looking for taxis. Feeling bold – feeling, indeed, luckier than anyone else in sight – he even considered taking one himself, but thrift prevailed. Money was important to Suzuki. He did not come from a rich family. As the commonness of his name suggested, he stemmed from a class which was once not allowed to bear a name at all. His grandfather, after having passed by examination to the status of junior officer, had died on the battleship *Yamato*, leaving his son, Suzuki's father, to start the climb all over again, as a junior sales executive for one of the numerous, fiercely competing electrical appliance companies which had burgeoned in Japan after the war. In order to become a senior sales executive, Suzuki's father had worked himself to mental exhaustion. The company had been generous and kept him at half pay as a consultant, but for all the years of Suzuki's education, times had been hard. The pressure to do well on his family's behalf had been the governing force of Suzuki's life for as far back as he could remember. As a recruit for the bureaucracy he was being given his London pay and living allowance in *yen*, which meant, because of the favourable exchange rate, that he was earning well. But much of what he made he would have to take home. He did not resent this. He had no great material ambitions beyond the glittering, almost unimaginable prospect of possessing, one day, an apartment in Tokyo.

To this end he had begun a special bank account, which at the moment had pathetically little in it, but anything he might earn as a writer would go into it too, and who knew if it would not eventually swell to the required magnitude? The thought of that place of his own made parsimony voluptuous. Suzuki enjoyed managing the details of his living arrangements. When he got back to his room, the contrast between it and the girl's flat he had just left was as if a videotape of an explosion had been run backwards. All the furniture was, of course, Western style, but his belongings were arranged with an accuracy which he was careful to disturb only on purpose, and always with a view to restoring harmony as soon as possible. Ideally the disturbance itself should be orderly. That very night he sat down to write to his sponsor, Shimura-*san*, the editor in the great publishing house who had first spotted Suzuki's talent when he was still a schoolboy. Shimura-*san* had encouraged Suzuki's writings while he was at Tōdai and had arranged for their publication in the professional magazines. In Japan, the magazines are where the business of literature is principally carried on. A début in the magazines requires sound management. Shimura-*san* had shown, on Suzuki's behalf, a combination of forbearance and tactical certitude which his protégé would ever afterwards regard as a model. When Suzuki arranged his sheets of paper on the desk and began to write to his protector, he was as concentrated as if entranced. A Western observer would have been justified in thinking that this must be a monk in his cell. The impression of monastic asceticism was abetted by the shrine-like arrangement of photographs on the sideboard. Suzuki's personal photographs – his mother, his sister, and, from happier days, his father – were displayed in small silver frames on the bedside table. On the sideboard, however, in larger frames spaced carefully on a white cloth, were the photographs of his heroes. Shimura-*san* was there. So was Kawabata: the photograph had been taken in the year he was awarded the Nobel Prize, yet he was unsmiling. Equally grave was Matsushita, ancient head of the Matsushita group of companies, the great man whose capacity for long-term planning had done so much for Japan's industrial rebirth. Also present were Admiral Yamamoto and Prince Saionji. The inclusion of Herbert von Karajan might have seemed inappropriate at first glance, but there was no Japanese equivalent for a master international musician with such a huge industrial capacity and so long a career. The common factor among Suzuki's heroes was productivity over a long period and wisdom in old age. World fame was also a consideration, although Matsushita, compared with the flamboyant Morita of Sony, was a reclusive figure, and Prince Saionji's name was known only inside Japan, and then mainly to historians. Politically isolated, his power sapped by the machinations of a cabinet increasingly under the sway of the military, Saionji, in those nightmarish last years of the 1930s, had never ceased to argue against the folly of a war with the Western powers. Admiral Yamamoto was there for the same reason: not for planning that brilliant feat of arms, the attack on Pearl Harbour, but for bravely having given his opinion in advance that a war against the Western democracies must eventually be lost. If Saionji and Yamamoto had been listened to, the tragedy might not have occurred. Suzuki admired these men, not so much for having persevered in a lost cause as for having been right, for having judged the situation correctly. The war party had so arranged matters that the Emperor had been unable to hear the advice of his wise men. Suzuki could think of nothing more perilous than that degree of hermeticism. He himself would have known little about Japan's path to military disaster if Shimura-*san* had not told him. Japanese school textbooks were almost impenetrably bland on the subject. Most of Suzuki's contemporaries knew little about their country's turbulent recent history and cared less. Though Suzuki sometimes envied them their equilibrium, he was in no doubt that it was dangerous. He was grateful for having been saved from ignorance, and most of the gratitude he owed to Shimura-*san*, who incarnated the benefits of stating the case frankly. So in his letter to Shimura-*san* he mentioned the girl. Announcing his intention of being careful, he left the way open for his mentor to admonish him, or even warn him off. Suzuki might not act on the advice, but he wanted to hear it.

Early the following week, Suzuki also mentioned the girl

to Rochester-*san*, not because he wanted the journalist's advice – in most respects, that had proved good for nothing – but because he wanted to see if her name meant anything, beyond the renown earned by its original holder. Rochester-*san* said that he was ignorant in the area of what he called 'acne mags', but that it was not unknown, nowadays, for performers in popular music and its attendant fields to take an already famous name. There had been a Tom Jones and an Engelbert Humperdinck. There was, of course, Madonna. Soon, no doubt, there would be a Jesus Christ. Also, apparently, it was now common for minor cultural journalists in the fashion magazines to have names like Coleridge, Wordsworth and even Shakespeare. Suzuki had obtained his own copy of one of the magazines featuring an article by Jane Austen. He showed it to Rochester-*san* and asked his opinion. Rochester-*san* began reading it with obvious reluctance but after a while looked interested, and even started to nod with admiration. 'She can write very well, this girl. *Taihen joju imas*. Is that how you say very good?'

'*Taihen jōzu desu*. Almost right.'

'Her style's not very well organised. All over the place like the mad woman's excreta. But she's got a turn of phrase.'

'What was that about the mad woman again?' asked Suzuki, suddenly on the alert.

'All over the place like the mad woman's excreta. I got that from an Australian newspaper proprietor. Good, isn't it? *Wakarimasu ka?*'

'*Wakarimashita*,' said Suzuki, meaning that he had understood. Plainly Rochester-*san* was keen to get on with the lesson. Suzuki did not have to feign approval of his pupil's diligence. Rochester-*san* had been doing some homework and would perhaps one day be able to sustain a simple conversation. Whether he would ever get far with his reading was a different matter. He was still reading everything in the Roman alphabet and could construe the phonetic scripts only with difficulty. He seemed incapable of retaining more than a dozen *kanji* characters. If he learned a new one, he forgot one he knew already. Also some of what he taught in return was so specialised that Suzuki doubted its value.

'My editor plays snooker,' said Rochester-*san*, 'but I'm *snookered*. You see the difference?' Suzuki did, but couldn't see its relevance. They were standing on the balcony gazing down into the evening. In a field of lights, a tower said TELECOM. Suzuki politely failed to notice the embarrassing moisture in his interlocutor's eye. 'Chin chin,' said Rochester-*san*, after refilling both their glasses. Since hearing that '*chinchin*' was one of the Japanese words for 'penis', Rochester-*san* had taken to saying it at every opportunity, invariably supplying his own laughter.

Talking to Rochester-*san*, however, was less of a trial than it had been. Suzuki was able to shift to automatic pilot while he thought about Austen-*san*. In his mind he had now begun to call her by her name. It seemed that she had some title to it. She was a writer after all. To his description of himself, Suzuki could add another attribute: he knew a promising young female English writer who dressed in the punk style, had large breasts, and had kissed him.

Next night after work he walked to her flat to keep their appointment. Once again she was not in when he pressed the button. This time, however, she did not turn up late. She did not turn up at all. He was outside the door for several hours and had an embarrassing conversation with a policeman. People who let themselves in or out of the door made it very clear that he should not try to go in. He did not want to. He would have liked to eliminate the possibility that she was up there in the flat dead by her own hand, but he could not visualise the scene by which he would obtain access. If he had told the policeman that a girl might have committed suicide up there, and the policeman had broken in and found that a girl *had* committed suicide up there, would not he, Suzuki, be a prime suspect on a charge of murder? He had better reasons, however, for not raising the alarm. Fears for her life had been in his mind since long before he saw her scars. The way she leafed through a book was enough to raise doubt about her chances of survival. But somehow on this occasion he was reasonably confident that she had simply missed the appointment. Such behaviour was, after all, even more part of her pattern than self-injury was. She would do nothing so dramatically apposite as to give an appointment to an admirer and then fail to answer her door because she was lying dead behind it. She was just not there. That Suzuki now recognised himself as her admirer only added to his irritation. Next day he called again and there was still no answer. This time he waited only an hour, always alert for the first signs of the patrolling policeman. Why had he not asked her for her telephone number? Her phone might be working again by now. Why had she not given him the number automatically? Why had he not read the number from the telephone in her flat and noted it down later? The card he had given her as a preliminary courtesy had his telephone numbers for both work and home on it. So why had she not rung? He was not sure his pride could take another fruitless early evening walk, which anyway he could not undertake until the day after tomorrow, because tomorrow he had another scheduled session with Rochester-*san*. Perhaps he could go to her place again after that was finished, but it would be late, and he might arrive simultaneously with the policeman. It was a dilemma.

Next day Jane Austen resolved it. As if having beamed down from a space-ship, she appeared in the bookshop during the most busy period, at mid-day. Instead of striking her in the face, Suzuki found himself agreeing to call on her that evening. He explained that he would not be able to arrive until the middle of the evening because he had one of his regular exchange language lessons first, and those he never missed. She said that she might have to go out in the later part of the evening, but at least they could spend an hour together. She intimated that it was very important that they did, because she had a lot to tell him that she couldn't tell him here. Suzuki could endorse the latter part of that opinion. His colleagues were going discreetly frantic as they tried to deal with the customers while he spent an age closeted between the high shelves in colloquy with this apparition of a female. The way she addressed most of her remarks to him over her shoulder while pulling books at random from the shelves and stuffing them back upside down did not help. Further reminded, by the very way she did this, of her compulsively eccentric timekeeping, Suzuki had a horrible premonition of himself arriving at her front door half an hour after she had left it. No, his appointment with Rochester-*san* would have to be cancelled. He told Austen-*san* that he would be there straight after work.

'Yeah,' she said. 'Well, then. Now that you've *finally* finished wanking.' Still manifesting disdain – she actually put her nose in the air – for how long it had taken to persuade him into a reasonable course of action, she pushed approximately between the other customers and left the shop. It was some time before there was a sufficient lull for Suzuki to ring Rochester-*san* and call off the appointment. Rochester-*san* accepted the situation without a trace of rancour. Several times, when obliged to leave suddenly for the Middle East or somewhere, he had made similar calls to Suzuki. But Suzuki disliked the sensation of squandering even a small part of his moral advantage. In his mental account book he had an entry in the debit column. Though the choice had been his, inevitably he felt sharp resentment against Austen-*san*. The flaring access of animus soon faded, but he still carried the hot embers when he reached her doorbell, and the embers crackled back to life when the doorbell was not answered. Suzuki had his executive briefcase with him and wondered whether, to help relieve his feelings, it might not be wise to put the briefcase flat on the ground, kneel beside it, take a deep breath, and punch a hole through it. But in a remarkably short time, for her, Austen-*san* showed up. Once again she was carrying two clinking plastic carrier bags, which he once again, as gallantry dictated, took from her. She, with a great show of retaliatory independence, took his briefcase.

'What *is* this? It's *heavy*. Have you got your wank mags in this?' She was in her standard black uniform, her areas of revealed skin looking even more abruptly candid than he had remembered. The notice on the back wall of the lift had been painted out with black paint. Presumably it was the same graffiti artist who had employed the newly primed display area to supply, this time in white paint, a further message which went into more, and more explicit, detail than its predecessor. Still absorbed in what he had just read, Suzuki had followed Austen-*san* into her flat before he noticed that she did not have his briefcase with her. 'Go and *get* it, then.' She spoke as if he had inconvenienced her, instead of the other way about. Suzuki pressed the button to call the lift. When the lift came, it did not have his briefcase in it. As he rode down in the lift he reflected that he would have to get used, not only to wasting a lot of time waiting for her, but to wasting a lot of the time he actually spent with her. When the lift reached the ground floor, the briefcase was not there either. Luckily, when he ran out into the street, the two little boys who were playing with it were still in view. They gave it back to him only when he frowned, a sight which made one of them – the larger one, strangely enough – burst into tears. Some man who was perhaps related to the boys shouted instructions from a balcony. 'Bugger off!' was the only instruction Suzuki understood clearly. Head back, Suzuki focused on the distant figure. The man looked large, bald and angry. 'Garn, get out of it, you fuckin' slant-eyed git! Sod off!'

Whatever it meant, it was a command Suzuki was glad to obey. He was back inside the lift before the man could reach the street. He realised that there was no point asking Austen-*san* why she had left the briefcase behind. The reason was obvious. She had put the briefcase down in order to leave both hands free for the challenging business of pushing the button, and then had simply forgotten to pick it up again. When he knocked on her closed door, it was a couple of minutes before she opened it, and then she looked at him as if wondering who he was. Is she acquainted, Suzuki found himself wondering, with any other Japanese men of my age, height and general appearance? 'What a *wanker*,' she told the wall. 'The *fuss* you make about things. Are you all like that?'

'Are who all like what?'

'Japs. Wankers. Are you *all* like that? I mean *really*.'

But she must have felt at least a residual sense of obligation, because she gave herself to him almost immediately. Suzuki was pleasantly surprised to find that in respect of her person she was, by Western standards, scrupulously clean. The disorder of her surroundings had been misleading in that regard. Divested of her strange garments, she looked odd only at the wrists and in the vicinity of the head, where her spiky, dyed blonde coronet now emphasised that her face was of a disproportionately restricted area compared with the body below it. She verged on the hefty, rather like the Degas women Suzuki had so much and so many times admired at the museum in Ueno Park, but with the milky white skin of the Renoir women he had admired even more. On the skin of the Renoir women, however, you could see the streaks denoting the direction of the brush. Austen-*san*'s skin had the stillness of freshly fallen powder snow. Also, for all that her body was solidly made, her lower limbs were long and tapered, thus going some way towards fulfilling Suzuki's ideal of the Western womanly figure. Suzuki did not precisely expect every Western woman to be as elongated as the Princess of

Wales, but there could be no doubt that, viewed generally, the Western female figure differed from the Japanese female figure in ways which Suzuki could not blame himself for being interested in, since Japanese women thought the same.

In the previous generation, Japanese women had been known to compensate for their low-slung flat bottoms by purchasing padded pantie-girdles with a high curvature built in. In the new generation, Japanese females, like Japanese males, had markedly shown the benefits of a diet whose protein content had been steadily increasing since the Occupation. The steady increase had led to a quantum jump. Legs had grown straighter and longer. But in general, for both sexes, the Japanese figure still was, and would remain, balanced equally around the middle. The Western figure carried its centre of gravity much higher. The women, especially, were less earthbound.

Austen-*san*, although she was as tall as Suzuki, was not especially tall for a Western woman. She was even a trifle chunky. She still struck Suzuki as ethereal, an effect helped by her angelic texture. He revelled in her. The only anxiety was induced by the circumstance that there seemed to be nothing she would not let him do, so he could not eliminate the possibility from his mind that he was somehow failing her. Yet she seemed to be as excited as he was. Even though there was never any detectable evidence that she was experiencing an orgasm, there was equally never any detectable evidence that she would not soon do so. She seemed to be always on the point of crisis. Finally Suzuki decided that he had better put off that matter to be decided later. He could wait no longer. He closed his eyes and said the informal Japanese word for yes. To English ears it sounds exactly like a grunt. When he opened his eyes again, Austen-*san* was smiling. For once she was looking straight at him. Her teeth were exquisite. Suzuki was glad that they would never be painted black. Here was no *geiko*. This was a free woman of the West. Suzuki had sailed all the way to the heart of the secret.

'Well, then,' said Austen-*san*, 'We're a bit less of a wanker in *this* department, *aren't* we?'

From that moment, even in his mind, he called her by her first name, Jane. Usually she didn't call him anything, but if forced to do so she called him Suzuki, because his first name, Akira, was more than she could manage. Anyway, she said, she liked the sound of Suzuki. 'It sounds dozy. Dozy and cosy. Cosy nookie, that's you. *That's* what *you* are.' As he lay in her arms after they had made love, she would baby him. Many Japanese men are, in childhood, weaned late, and for them, in adult life, such affectionate treatment is powerfully soothing. Suzuki was grateful and showed his gratitude by tender caresses. These, she assured him, had been rare in her life. Between Jane Austen and Akira Suzuki, such peaceful interludes were to become the central, connecting thread of their affair as it stretched into the summer. Perhaps on that first evening they both had a premonition of this consoling fact, because they grinned at each other from short range, less like stunned novices than like established lovers who have been familiar with each other's bodies for a long time.

Jane climbed into a crushed but clean navy blue cotton bathrobe printed with hibiscus. It looked better on her than it had on the floor, but no less crumpled. Yet Suzuki, sitting cross-legged on the bed, was aesthetically well pleased as he

46

watched her through the frame of the kitchen doorway while she set about ransacking the shopping bags, pouring drinks, and laying out the ingredients of a possible salad. As on the first evening, Suzuki was handed a wine glass full to the brim with vodka. Some of it splashed over the brim and soaked his hand. As he watched her slicing tomatoes, he wondered if she had ever really tried to commit suicide at all. She might have done all that to herself while preparing a light snack. Yet there was a transparency to her that he admired. Her body carried no blemishes except those she had put there herself, by violence. Her hairstyle and make-up were merely an extended version of the self-obliterating damage she had done with the razor. Her voluptuously curved outline was purely drawn. If she was incapable of propelling it into graceful movement, he would either have to imagine graceful movements on her behalf, or else simply try to accept what he saw. He tried to imagine her in Japanese traditional dress, slowly and meticulously laying out the utensils for the tea ceremony. The thought was instantly dispelled when she tore a lettuce to pieces without looking at it. He could hear the lettuce scream for mercy.

Daringly clad in nothing except his shirt and underpants, Suzuki sat down opposite his hostess at the tiny table in the kitchenette. Jane now began to tell him her news. It was no more coherent than usual. Nor, though laughter was interspersed, was it really any more light-hearted. She had gone to Paris to see the singer who until recently had lived here in the flat with her. His name was Ron. Apparently the fix she was in was really all his fault, the bastard. He had run up a huge phone bill making long calls all over the world, the cunt. That was why they had cut the phone off, the wankers. The big advantage about that was that the bank manager couldn't make any more threatening phone calls, the wanker cunt bastard. Careful not to betray, with his facial expression, that he was undertaking a manoeuvre equivalent to making a U-turn across the central divide of a super highway, Suzuki suggested that he might be able to help her a little in the matter of money. Jane made her customary dismissive gesture as of someone trying to demoralise a wasp. It seemed that the article about Japan would restore her fortunes overnight. Her only mistake had been to promise it to one of the acne mags. But its editor had behaved so badly, pestering her all the time, that she had decided to give it to the colour magazine of one of the Sunday newspapers. She asked Suzuki for a few trendy names to put into the piece. When it emerged that Suzuki was a writer himself, Jane suggested – insisted, in fact – that she should interview him and modify the article so that the interview became the core of it. Suzuki would have been flattered if he had really believed that there was anything to modify. He was fairly certain, by now, that the article did not exist in any form. Apart from her mishaps, which were all real enough to touch, her life was totally unreal. Suzuki wondered how her affair with him would eventually be classified: fantastic, or mistaken? He was in a long way over his head, yet he had never seen so clearly. When she told him that her singing friend Ron was bisexual, Suzuki felt a thrill of fear so sharply defined that it had a cutting edge, like a short sword slashing his stomach open with its long, withdrawing stroke. 'I'm the only woman he can go to bed with. It's often like that. Pooves who've never had a woman in their lives try it once, with me. I hope *you're* not one. Are there any Japanese woofters?'

Suzuki was smiling, but in his mental account book he had turned to a fresh page and entered a possible debt that might have to be cancelled with his life. By rights he should have put on his trousers, bowed low and walked straight to the hospital he had noticed just down the road. He restricted himself to telling her that she must never have intercourse with any of these men again. He forbade it. 'Oo, aren't we *masterful?*' Jane asked the refrigerator.

So they went back to bed. Jane made noises about having to go out. These were soon replaced by other noises she made; noises Suzuki liked. Like the Japanese lover of the blonde American princess in *Big Comic*, Suzuki was spending a lot of time with his head buried in his work, but he did not complain. If he had, the complaints would have been muffled. She made no grand gestures of awarding him the freedom of her body. She simply seemed to expect these things. He soon learned that it was up to him to decide when he had had enough. When he once again gave the monosyllabic signal that he had, she patted his forehead maternally and departed to the bathroom. He heard the clunking sound of a slab of porcelain being shifted. Surely not even she was so erratic as to dismantle the water-closet simply by sitting on it? She came back with a small plastic bag from which she produced the makings of marijuana cigarettes.

'This is Ron's stuff. I don't usually have it, in case the council breaks in. I don't actually smoke it, actually. I used to once, before I got into drugs. You know, *real* drugs. But after that, I didn't smoke it any more. What's the *point?* So

I just have the occasional smoke, because if it doesn't matter, it doesn't matter if you *do*, does it? So I *smoke*: so what?'

'Yes.'

Suzuki had smoked a marijuana cigarette while at university and found it quite interesting. His instinct now was to run downstairs, find the attentive local policeman, and place himself under arrest. He was about to become engaged in doing absolutely the last thing an ambitious young Japanese visitor to a Western country should ever do. On future occasions, he would forbid her even to raise the subject. But this was his night of madness. Tonight he was in the Floating World.

'Ooh,' said Jane, after taking, holding, and only partly expelling a deep drag from the second cigarette. 'I wish we had some *drugs*.' His share of the first cigarette had left Suzuki feeling odd, but not so odd that he did not find what she said even odder. If this wasn't a drug, what was it? Luckily all the active ingredient was soon gone. There had been more than enough of it to stimulate Jane into a version of her usual monologue more wide-ranging, and less connected, than ever. She railed against her parents in a way Suzuki found impossible to understand. According to her, they were wealthy landowners who had reacted with cruel incomprehension when she would not conform. She did not know which of them she hated more. But she hated the manager of the band more than both of them. Japan was where he had started to sabotage her, in fact. The lead singer was his boyfriend and together they had grown jealous of the attention she was getting. 'I mean I would come out and the whole audience would just go, *ungh*! You know what I mean?

I mean it was that kind of thing. It was that kind of *experience*. I know it's past it and everything to say experience but it really *was*. They would just go *ungh*!'

She remembered Japan clearly. She had, she said, a natural affinity with Japan. That was why she had been chosen to write this article. She had seen a lot of Japan. There was a big hall in Tokyo. And there was a big hall in another place. And in Tokyo there was a place with a lot of lights, like Times Square in New York only better. With a big TV set and lights hitting the clouds. She knew what it was called. What was it called?

'Shinjuku,' said Suzuki.

'See? I *knew* that. That's why they got me to write this *terrific* article.'

'You,' said Suzuki dreamily, 'are all over the place like the mad woman's etcetera.'

'Where did you get that? Nobody says that.'

'The man to whom I give lessons told me.'

'*Nobody* says that. I'll tell you what, though.'

'What?'

'I know a few *guys* you could give lessons to.' She dug a knuckle into his clearly defined abdominal muscles. 'You're just an old slag, aren't you? You're just an old sex-mad Jap *slag*.'

She smiled into his eyes. For what seemed an age he had her undivided attention. Then she looked sideways at the wall, leaned forward and kissed him.

FOUR

BREATHING HARD, Suzuki lay in the double leg-thrust Nautilus machine after completing fifteen repetitions at 285 pounds. Just because of what he had eaten and drunk in Jane's presence, he would have been keen enough to get to the gymnasium. There was also the question of the terrible risk he was running from the medical viewpoint. Exercise might not be of much value against microbes or viruses but if a prepared body had a better chance of fighting them off then he did not intend to let the chance go. His thighs were trembling. Jane had been missing for more than a week. For all he knew she was already in hospital or dead. There was no means of contacting her. The arrangement, such as it was, was that she would show up in the bookshop when she returned from wherever it was that she had gone. Or she could telephone. The name Ron had kept recurring in her explanations of how her financial crisis was to be temporarily alleviated, prior to the permanent cure which would be effected when the Sunday newspaper's colour magazine paid her a small fortune for her article on Japan. Suzuki was alarmed to find how thoroughly his relief that she was out of his hair was undercut by his sense of loss.

There was also the sense of panic, which an intensified programme at the gymnasium helped to keep under control. A letter from Shimura-*san* had arrived. While not precisely a grim warning, it reminded Suzuki, as if he needed reminding, that by contracting an intimacy with any kind of Western woman, let alone a mere girl of the *demi monde* like this one, he was putting his destiny into needless jeopardy. 'Even with the benefit of all possible foresight', wrote Shimura-*san*, 'the unknown must necessarily play a leading role in human life. Judiciousness already entails risk. Actually to embrace risk is the privilege only of artistic genius.' Shimura-*san* said, as he had said before, that he had high hopes of Suzuki's literary talent. There could be no doubt that an artist must, indeed would without prompting, follow the inclinations of his desires beyond the limits dictated by what would seem immediate self-interest.

'You have often heard me speak of Charles de Gaulle,' – wrote Shimura-*san* – 'that great figure in the history of his country's reconstruction, and a worthy model, it has always seemed to me, for us to emulate in the reconstruction and advancement of our own. In his memoirs, which I urge you to read one day, he quotes one of his own mentors, Chamfort, to this effect: "Those who were reasonable have survived. Those who were passionate have lived." It is a pregnant distinction, is it not? Among all the promising young men who have come my way, it is you, Suzuki Akira, who must live. But you must also survive. So pursue this relationship only so far as it opens you up to useful experience, and not a centimetre further.'

Thinking of this admonition now, Suzuki rose from the machine with a sigh, towelled down its backrest politely even though he had left scarcely a trace of sweat, and moved towards the next machine on his programme. It was a quiet time on Sunday afternoon and the gymnasium was almost empty. A beautiful honey-blonde English girl with legs longer than the Tokyo tower was running on one of the treadmills. Her name was Lilian: a very hard word for Suzuki to pronounce. An English stockbroker and amateur heavyweight boxer named Lionel – an even harder word for Suzuki to pronounce – spent some time watching her appreciatively before turning to Suzuki and addressing him with a by now shop-worn pleasantry.

'Wotcher, Akira. How's your endurance? Awe rye?' Suzuki had worked out within the first week of joining the club that when the members made jokes about his endurance they were referring to the Japanese television programme of that name, extracts from which were broadcast on British television eked out with a facetious commentary by an Australian in lamentable physical condition. Though the mockery of his fellow members was hard to distinguish from racism, Suzuki did not particularly mind. His own opinion of its perpetrators could not be said to spring from feelings of racial inferiority. What bothered Suzuki about the enormous Lionel was the version of English he spoke. Only recently had Suzuki figured out that by the word 'wotcher' Lionel did not necessarily mean that there was some female nearby who merited being observed. He merely meant Hello. Suzuki was glad to have puzzled this out before today, when the close presence of a girl who certainly rewarded being watched would have confused the issue beyond salvation. Suzuki assured Lionel that his endurance was all right. Lionel, apparently satisfied, swaggered hugely off to where the speed ball was hanging. He tapped it with one fist so that it said *rat-tat*. He tapped it with both fists so that it said *rattata-tattata*. He took a deep breath and hit it for five minutes so that it sounded like a machine-gun. The treadmill, helplessly drawn towards the exquisite Lilian's finely muscled advancing legs, said *whump-whump-whump*. Lulled by these rhythms, Suzuki moved on to the abdominal machine, selected the right weight, adjusted the seat height, settled the pads against his shoulders, took a breath, and jack-knifed forward. He had not done half a dozen repetitions before he heard Lionel's voice behind him.

'Gettin' a bit of bowin' practice in, are we, Akira?' It was the other joke that Lionel always made. Plunging forward with his upper body, Suzuki smiled while expelling his breath. It was always a good moment when the second of Lionel's two jokes was over. Lionel wandered off to observe Lilian as she floated above the treadmill like a sprite running on a bubble. To watch her. For the millionth time, Suzuki wondered if he would ever come to terms with the English language. He was not entirely demoralised, however. He knew for a certainty why he felt so unsure. It was because of the uncertainty which he had, of his own volition, allowed into his life. He had expected to be able to contain the disturbing element more easily, but it threatened to contaminate areas the stability of which he had taken for granted. The possibility of infection was simply a gamble, potentially as devastating as losing at Russian roulette. All he could do was keep fit and hope.

Yesterday, however, feeling hungry on the way to the tube station after work, he had found himself purchasing an English chocolate bar. The confection had been called something like a

Kix or a Snax or a Drex: by now he had repressed the name. He only wished he could repress the aftertaste. Unwrapped, it had looked like a lump of excrement containing the remains of an only partly digested meal of nuts. That was what all those English sweetmeats looked like: dollops of excrement. Every newsagent had at least one wall lined with rack upon rack of brightly wrapped turds. Standing on the platform of St Paul's station with the partly peeled object in one hand and his executive briefcase in the other, Suzuki had gazed at that hellish dark banana, whose sickly sweet tip he had just bitten off, and suddenly wondered what chain of circumstances had led him to this pass. In every sense, the thing was in bad taste. He had had an immediate, incandescent vision of the cookie shop in the Ginza district where he went every week to buy a box of biscuits for his mother. The delicate texture of the pastel-coloured wrapping paper, the flourish with which the ribbon was tied, the look of the thin cookies in their serried ranks as they leaned back in the box – it was a congeries of remembered sense impressions, a symposium of subtleties that made, by comparison, the mess in his mouth feel as if a dog had voided its bowels on his tongue.

Upon his arrival, the eating habits of the English had caused Suzuki even more psychological disturbance than the ubiquitous litter and the universally bellicose level of verbal aggression. But he had learned to accept their disgusting ways with food, in the same way that Englishmen who visited Japan had to learn to accept, so he had been told, the way that Japanese men cleared their throats of phlegm. Suzuki had found learning not to hawk and spit far easier than learning how to eat the local nutriment, but after a decent interval he had begun to take the occasional quick lunch in the health food café near the bookshop. In Tokyo Suzuki had eaten in many a Western-style restaurant and like all Japanese people of his educational level he had learned Western table manners to a degree of delicacy which most Westerners evidently found pedantic. Suzuki did not feel at a loss in a London eating establishment. He simply felt appalled. Even in the most expensive restaurants, the insolence of the service was an offence and the sloppiness of the guests an affront. The health food café was at least nominally dedicated to serving good things. Mostly Suzuki would take twenty minutes in the back of the bookshop to eat a boxed lunch sent in from the local Japanese restaurant. But when he ate in the health food café he tried to relish the experience. He would tuck into a stoneware bowl full of multi-coloured salad and feel that he was living off the land, far inside the border of a foreign culture. Such an adventurous displacement was, however, as far as he was prepared to go. To find himself purchasing a chocolate bar – to find himself actually taking a bite out of a monolith of solidified ordure – was a sign that he had submitted himself to the grip of an elemental force. When the train had pulled in, Suzuki had been holding only the briefcase. The chocolate bar, rewrapped, was in the trash bin behind him, from which, no doubt, it would later be extracted by some tramp, for whom it would furnish the roughage of an evening meal.

The treadmill whined to a stop. Lilian lightly skipped backwards out of it, waved to him in a way which acknowledged his existence while betraying no anxiety at the prospect of separating herself from it, and covered the few steps to the far door with strides that barely touched the carpet, as if her pink leotard, cut high at the sides over her pearl-grey leggings, was lifting her with a force equal to her weight, plus a few ounces. She left a void. Suzuki found himself alone in the gymnasium. Glad to be unobserved, he moved to one of the exercise mats and stood on his hands. He lifted his left hand and touched its fingertips to his left thigh while tilting his body slightly to the right. He stood there on his right hand for fifteen seconds and then changed hands. Returning to a two-hand stand, he dived slowly out of it into a forward roll which ended with his legs splayed to each side, toes pointed. With both hands he pushed the floor away so that the extended straight line of his open legs was an inch above the mat. He leaned forward and lifted himself into another handstand, from which he walked over and walked away. Nobody could have seen him. Suzuki would not have wanted to draw attention to himself in this matter. At school he had done well in gymnastics. He had made only the second team at university and had eventually decided to give it up. If he had been truly excellent he might have gone on, but gymnastics in Japan had attained such a high standard, and boasted champions in such depth, that to be less than first rate meant that there was nothing to hope for except beneficial effects to one's personal health. Suzuki was not displeased that that part of his life was over. He had moved on. The life of the mind made demands to which the condition of his body could only be subservient.

In the empty dressing-room panelled with grey-painted metal lockers, Suzuki removed his sweat-shirt, socks and shoes, retaining only the shorts while he showered off the sweat. Actually Suzuki's body, unless hard pressed, hardly perspired at all, but the club standing orders said that the swimming-pool should not be entered without a shower first. Suzuki showered as thoroughly as if there had been a hidden camera. Then he climbed the steps to the swimming-pool, which he entered just as Lionel was leaving it. 'Wotcher, Akira. How's your endurance. Awe rye?' Lionel, having run the gamut of his jokes, had begun again. Lilian did not swim quite as well as she danced. She smiled at him as she forged past in a strong but rather wasteful breast stroke, her black Lycra-clad bottom gleaming like a dolphin with a split skull. She smiled at him again after she had climbed out of the pool, reached for her towel, and thereby offered him further revelations of how radiantly lissom the Western female body could be.

Suzuki waited until she had left the pool area altogether before he increased his pace. He had been quite a promising swimmer, too. Promising but not startling. Even had he been more talented, he would probably not have gone on with it. Japanese competitive swimming had reached its peak in the Fifties, when Shimura-*san*'s generation had been young. Shimura-*san*, indeed, had been the third swimmer in the Japanese 4 x 400 metres freestyle relay team at the Melbourne Olympics in 1956. Competition swimming had been the route of the Japanese nation's return to world prominence after the war. But soon the Australians, and then the Americans, had attained superiority. All other things being equal, dominance in the swimming-pool went to the physical type with the greater length of leg. The very factor which kept Japanese men supreme in gymnastics, their symmetrical equality of trunk and lower limb, set a limit to the leverage they could achieve in the water. Suzuki did not find this a matter of regret. He was proud of his people. Until recently he had been proud of himself. He had thought of himself as a cool customer.

In the absence of Jane he might have profited by paying renewed attention to his obligations. Normally he would have made such an adjustment without faltering. He would have made up for any hour of dissipation with two hours of dedicated work. But this time he found himself moongazing. He wrote a poem. It took him a long time. After writing out a fine copy with a brush on good paper, he translated it into English.

> As the cherry blossom
> After it has fallen
> Is scattered on the pavement by the wind
> So her life drifts –
> Appreciable only for a moment
> Which exists in movement.

Suzuki was up late for two nights working on the poem and could not call himself ecstatic with the result, to which he gave the title 'The Girl with Milk Skin'. Technically it was a breakthrough in his work. Strictly traditional in form, it yet contained elements of word music – for example, the deliberately placed interior rhyme of the words *kaze* (wind) and *naze* (cause, reason) – which could be attributed only to, and not necessarily justified by, Western influence. Transcribing the original language version of his poem into a letter to Shimura-*san*, Suzuki was trepidatious about what his mentor might think. The English language version he took along on his next visit to Rochester-*san*. Eager to make up to Rochester-*san* for having broken a date with him, Suzuki knew that the English journalist, who loved to give advice, would take delight in being consulted by his Japanese apprentice on the technicalities of English verse. Nor were Rochester-*san*'s admonitions and exhortations, when they had to do with literature and the arts, quite as useless as they were in other fields. In the field of *savoir faire*, the very area in which Rochester-*san* considered himself an expert, it was a miracle that he could get across the street alive. But he was a genuinely cultivated man, although even when it came to the arts he was so mercurial in his judgments, so effervescent in his enthusiasms, that Suzuki scarcely knew which of the multiplicity of suggested courses he was supposed to take. Suzuki was pleased, however, to be told that his conscious deployment of the words 'moment' and 'movement', though it would not be considered subtle by an informed critic, would not be considered clumsy either. He was displeased to be told that the long-range chime of 'pavement' and 'movement' was a startling achievement for someone writing in his second language. He was displeased because he had not planned it. It was a fluke. He confessed this, and was told that the sum total of such flukes amounted to a talent for writing English poetry.

'Don't go a bundle on the title, though,' said Rochester-*san*, apparently as an afterthought.

'Don't go a bundle?'

'I don't think it's quite right. Trouble is, milk has a skin of its own when it's been boiled or gone sour. Rather unfortunate associations.'

'Yes.'

'Call it "A Girl With Skin Like Milk" and you'll be OK. Because then it can only be *her* skin, do you see?'

'Yes. Now I do. I didn't before. You are always a great help in these things.'

It was not quite true. Always alert to the possibility of an invaluable free lesson about the nuances of the English language, Suzuki took in everything Rochester-*san* said, which was what was so exhausting about their relationship, because on larger issues so much of what Rochester-*san* said, after it had been taken in and examined, had to be thrown out again. Yet Suzuki could not deny that he had learned a lot from Rochester-*san*. Once having recovered from finding out how completely Galsworthy's reputation had collapsed, Suzuki had been gratified, while being given a tour of Rochester-*san*'s shelves, to be told many other literary names that he might follow up. He had been following some of them up ever since, although here again it was always necessary to discount Rochester-*san*'s spur of the moment enthusiasms and sort out what was essential. Suzuki had learned his first hard lesson in that regard when he had spent a week getting half-way through Morley Callaghan's *That Summer in Paris* before finding out that on the subject of writers in Paris he should have been reading, in the first instance, Ernest Hemingway and F. Scott Fitzgerald. Rochester-*san* was a bad teacher from that viewpoint. He knew everything himself, but couldn't remember how he had found out, so he made no allowance for the fact that his pupil would either have to proceed step by step or else retire bewildered. Suzuki's annoyance, however, was soon offset by his respect for Rochester-*san*'s undoubted erudition, remarkable over the whole range of the arts, and especially, as far as Suzuki could tell, profound in the area of Western music. On LP, cassette or compact disc, Rochester-*san* seemed to be in possession of every important recording ever made. Just the books on music filled a whole long wall. On the subject of Suzuki's hero Karajan, Rochester-*san* was irreverent but illuminating.

'Now's the time', said Rochester-*san*, 'to go for *das Wunder*'s early performances while they're coming out on cheap tapes.' It was later in the same evening. Suzuki had offered up his poem for praise and analysis. Now it was time for the retaliatory gift. Though Rochester-*san* was scarcely a model of sensitivity, it might just have been possible that he had realised, at some subconscious level, that Suzuki had done him an honour. Anyway, for once he spoke to the point, with comparatively few digressions. 'You see, the trouble with old Karajan is that he's so *bloody* convinced that music is made of *sound*, he can't leave well alone. He gets such a lush *sound* out of the Berlin Phil, – that's the Philharmonic, sorry, you might remember that one – gets such a bloody beautiful *sound* out of it, that when digital recording came along he couldn't resist the opportunity to make everything again. And then CD came along and he wanted to make everything *again*, do you see? Result is, all the older performances have started piling up in the back catalogue. So now you're starting to get them on cheap tapes. And some of them were simply *better* than anything he's likely to do now. Not just because he was younger, but because the limitations of the medium – no, better way of putting it, *the lack of opportunities to be indulgent beyond reasonable expectation*, that's it – kept him in line. Made him cleave to a more compact *line*. Better shape.

Less of the beautiful luxuriant sprawl and more of the tight vibrant *shape*. Like you. But we won't go into that. Because we can't, can we, my own lovely? Chin chin.'

Suzuki, as he had long ago learned to, smiled with the exact measure of polite regret which made Rochester-*san* feel that a Platonic romance was better than nothing. Rochester-*san* sank the rest of his brandy, stood up, poured them both another, settled back into his chair, and went on, so obviously loving the sound of his own voice that Suzuki felt pity for him, as for a child lasciviously rolling the products of its picked nose between finger and thumb. But the pity was more than balanced by respect. What a lot this man knew. Suzuki wanted to be knowledgeable, as he had once wanted to fly for Japan on the high bar. It would come. Listen and learn.

'Take that new *Rosenkavalier* of his,' Rochester-*san* went on. 'On CD it sounds unbelievable. Un-be-*liev*able. But when you listen to the trio in the last act, the dynamics have gone to pot.'

'Gone to pot?'

'Gone to the dogs. To buggery. Way of saying they've deteriorated. Like me, rather. Three *gorgeous* voices going absolutely nowhere. Put on his old Schwarzkopf set straight after it and the difference is enough to convince anybody that he should never, *ne-ver*, have conducted the thing again. Have you heard it, by the way? His first *Rosenkavalier* set? The one with Schwarzkopf and Christa Ludwig? No?'

Rochester-*san* found the tape, put it on the machine, and the evening proceeded. At first the sound seemed crowded to Suzuki. Japanese classical instrumentation was so sparse and pure that he, who was no musician, could almost tell if a *shamisen* was being played in sunlight or in shadow. Western music always sounded dense at first hearing. But as Rochester-*san* rewound the tape to play the same passage over and over, Suzuki gradually sorted out the three voices. That was what he was here for: to sort out the voices. Rochester-*san* was helping to give him the West. As the clumsy Englishman turned down the lights to make the atmosphere conform more closely to his amorous dreams, the many diodes of the National Panasonic audio stack lit up like the eyes of nocturnal insects. It was how Japan lived: by reading the world's mind and helping it to the realisation of what it wished.

What Suzuki wished was less easily divined, by him at any rate. He was prepared, in his mental account book, to offset the inconvenience his new English mistress would cause him against the experience he would gain, not to mention the pleasure. But the account book lacked, as it were, a time-table. There was no means of knowing when Jane would turn up. The only time she called him on the telephone, she called his home number while he was at the bookshop. How could she possibly not realise that he would be at work during the hours of daylight? Did she think he was like her, waking in the middle of the day, not even knowing whether it was day or night without first looking out of the window? Shimura-*san* had once told him that all egomaniacs are like that: they think that all other people are like them. But Suzuki, at this stage, still found it hard to believe that the girl could be quite so disorganised. It went without saying that she could be so inconsiderate of the havoc she would cause by calling when he was out. She was not to know that his land-lady would be so hostile. He therefore did not blame Jane for the low-pitched but remorseless tirade with which the woman greeted him when he got home one evening. 'A Miss Austen rang.' That was the start of it. 'She sounded very strange to me. She sounded very angry that you weren't here. She used some very uncouth words. I can't be having that, Mr Suzy.' There was a lot more at the same steady tempo. Suzuki nodded and occasionally declined his head deferentially, halfway between a nod and a bow. He wondered if his landlady had not grown to like these signs of deference and had begun to contrive situations in which she might extract them from him. Though always dressed in a manner which suggested that she had either recently got out of bed or would soon get into it, she was well-proportioned in a middle-aged way and moved with surprising grace for someone whose vocal output was so brutal.

Suzuki did not blame her for calling him Mr Suzy. It was an improvement on what she had called him at first: Mr Jacuzzi. He himself had trouble pronouncing her name, a minefield of l's and th's. Ethel Thelwell. It took him an eternity. But beyond their linguistic estrangement there was undoubtedly an element, on her part, of conscious malice. Why did she take guests, if she was so irritated by the duties of being a hostess? It was a mystery to him, like the aggressively bad service in railway cafeterias, the drifts of rubbish in the streets, and the telephone-boxes that looked as if they had been bombed with phosphorus. These, he had noticed, were slowly being replaced with a new model public telephone unit which appeared to have been machined out of a single block of tungsten. It was a wise capitulation to the inevitable. Here, public property was the eternal victim in a war of attrition, whose patient aggressor, strangely, was the public itself. Suzuki was continually mystified by a society which featured so much open hostility in its everyday life yet so rarely came to blows. The rhythm of life in his own country was more spasmodic. Everything was done to avoid confrontation of any kind. Then, when an unkind word was spoken, there was no recourse except to tie a water-soaked bandanna around one's mouth, cram a crash helmet on to one's head, and fight.

FIVE

PERHAPS THERE WAS something to be said for a way of life in which bad thoughts could be made explicit without regrettable physical consequences. On the day when Jane once again materialised in the shop, Suzuki had the urge to stride across and swear at her. He considered this an improvement on the urge to stride across and throttle her. He had become Westernised. In the event, he did not even swear. He was too pleased. Also he was stunned. As usual she was in the art book section, but this time she was smoking a cigarette. The precious book about Japanese designs and advertising campaigns was once again in her careless hands, with the additional hazard that she was dropping ash into the valley between its open pages before impatiently leafing on and doing the same thing again. Suzuki arrived at her shoulder and with his voice damped down to a considerate murmur he aimed a message at where her ear would have been if it had not moved.

'You are an amazing woman.'

'Do you really think so, Sue?' she cried out, apparently delighted. 'You're not just saying that because you're a randy old slag?'

'I meant you are amazing because you return here only to destroy that book. The book resists you but you do not give up. You return always with new weapons. Now you bring fire.'

'Yeah. I started smoking again.'

'You can afford to do it?'

'It helps me stop worrying about money. I mean I couldn't give a *fuck* about money, you know that. But the man from the bank sent a *man* around, and he keeps *waiting* for me . . .'

Suzuki inwardly sighed with compassion at the thought of this latest recruit to the ranks of men who spent their lives waiting for Jane. He visualised a huge army stretching away into the distance, with himself at the head of it, wearing the uniform of General MacArthur. Having extracted from her a faithful promise that she would absolutely, without the possibility of failure, actually be there when he came to call after work that evening, he managed to get her out of the shop. She zig-zagged into the distance.

What he did next amazed him. A full half of the half hour he took for lunch he spent in the bank extracting two hundred and fifty pounds from his special fund. He couldn't believe he was doing it. He told himself that it was a calculated risk. The distant prospect of his own place in Tokyo might even be brought closer. This gesture would bring her near; he would get to know her better; their affair would thus make even deeper modifications to his essential self, ensuring more adventurous art works, a more resounding success, and thus a bigger flat. He could see it now: a split-level maisonette like Mishima's, with those wonderful Corbusier and Mies van de Rohe leather chairs. He tried to concentrate on its details. He very much wanted those leather chairs. The brute reality in the life of the typical young Japanese bureaucrat was that he could hardly afford to buy anything, even those home-grown products for which his country was famous. Japan was a prosperous country but its people were not. Suzuki did not enjoy Lionel's jokes but he enjoyed them better than hearing Lionel and his fellow arbitrageurs discussing the performance details of their Porsche 928S's and 6-series BMWs. Suzuki would get the Nobel prize before he could afford such a car. If he was very lucky, he might eventually own the sort of Toyota sports car that Lionel had traded in on the way to his first Porsche 944. Suzuki was not a materialist. He was spiritual about material things. He could taste their beauty in his mind. Only money could buy them, and the place to keep them. To contemplate risking even a small proportion of his precious money was like hacking at the rope by which he hung suspended from his future. Yet now the money was folded into an envelope, the envelope was in his pocket, and he was back in the shop counting the minutes before it closed. Japanese girls were shopping for the kind of Japanese comic books specifically aimed at Japanese girls: compendiums two inches thick with covers of ivory, mint green and rioting pink script. One or two of the girls were extremely pretty. Two or three of them actually. Why couldn't he get interested in one of *them*? There was an expression in English about money burning a hole in your pocket. It stopped short of the mark. This kind of money burned a hole in your chest.

Striding the well-worn path to where she lived, he got his first few sentences ready. It was a familiar process. Beyond a certain point a conversation in one's second language was not controllable, but it couldn't even start unless you had the first few exchanges well covered. Suzuki practised saying: 'I would be privileged to help you with your financial problem.' He changed 'problem' to 'difficulty' and found it no less difficult, so he changed it back to 'problem'. Mouthing the words, he was almost knocked down by a small Honda van, which bounced to a halt with squealing brakes. 'Fucking chink git!' cried the driver. 'Whyncha get back to China then? Cross-eyed cunt.'

'Thank you,' said Suzuki, acknowledging his fault. The driver, mollified, pressed on. Suzuki arrived at Jane Austen's front door and pressed the entryphone button. At first nothing happened, but what happened afterwards was truly startling. It was still nothing. Being almost killed by the little Honda van had been mildly depressing. Jane's not answering her bell brought him close to despair. He hung his head, a mourner at his own funeral. Time passed. Without looking at the sky, he sensed it growing ever so slightly darker. Late afternoon was shading into the long twilight of a summer evening. At last he had enough energy to move his head. He looked along the street to the left, wondering if she would arrive from that direction, always supposing that she arrived at all. He looked along the street to the right. A familiar figure loomed. It was the man who had shouted at him from the balcony on the occasion of his briefcase having been misappropriated. This time Suzuki did not have his briefcase with him, which was lucky, because the man and his two equally large friends looked very aggressive. 'Ear's a fuckin' chink what was fuckin' rhand wiv aagh kids,' said the man. 'Ear! Chink! Watch it! Ya got vat? Juss watch it. Rye?'

Suzuki, wanting to tell the man there had been a mistake, perhaps unwisely attempted an air of colloquial ease.

'You,' said Suzuki, 'are all over the place like the mad woman's excreta.'

'Get old of is arms while I bash the cunt,' said the man.

'Nut the wanker,' said one of the other men.

'Come on China,' said the third man, moving behind Suzuki, 'Time for bye-byes, you pox-eyed nig-nog.'

Suzuki was in trouble. He would find it very hard to get out of this situation without serious damage being caused. He leaned forward and tapped the man behind him gently in the stomach with the heel of his left foot – not an easy blow to inflict with delicacy unless the shoe has been removed. Meanwhile the first man's clenched fist was passing overhead, opening the arch of the armpit to a relatively easy knuckle thrust, but because Suzuki had only one foot to balance on he was obliged to hit harder than he would have liked. As the man behind him and the first man in front of him both fell with relative lack of force to the pavement, Suzuki would have preferred to step aside. He had barely enough time, however, to regain a two-footed stance. So he simply could not avoid hurting the second man in front of him, whose kick would have made contact if Suzuki had not caught it with his right hand and moved the offending foot briskly upwards. The man's head hit the pavement with a crack that could be heard above the shrieks emitted by the other two men as they lay writhing. Suzuki prayed that no fracture of the skull had been inflicted. He bent to inspect the immobile man's head. There was no blood. The breathing seemed normal. 'What's this, then?' said the policeman, showing his usual uncanny ability to materialise just when he could be of least help.

Suzuki was eventually believed when he said he had been more intent on restoring order than perpetrating grievous bodily harm. The policeman took the point that Suzuki's high grade in karate meant that the scuffle would have had a very different result if his intention had been other than self-defence. But the discussion took a long time and might well have resulted in the unthinkable disaster of official proceedings if Jane had arrived earlier. As it was, the three local men – the one with the smitten skull now conscious and moaning low like the other two – had already agreed that Suzuki's insane act of aggression should be regarded as sufficiently punished. Jane loudly advised Suzuki to kick them all again but by that time the policeman had put his notebook away. Even more loudly, Jane advised Suzuki to kick the policeman. Suzuki was already escorting her firmly to her door.

'You're not going to let him get away with *that!*' wailed Jane. 'He should have slung them all in the nick. You've been *discriminated against*! Hey, copper! You're a racist wan . . .'

Suzuki gagged her as gently as he could with one hand while he fished out her keys with the other. Having got her safely through the door, he was somehow not surprised that she tried to seduce him in the lift. She was shiny-eyed with excitement. 'Ooh, Sue, I *saw* you. They were flying around like *aeroplanes*. You're so *hard*, aren't you? You're just a hard old macho *stud*.' They fell through the door of her flat on to the floor. With her ankles around his neck and his nose in her stereo equipment, Suzuki wondered why he had come to England in order to live out scenes from a Japanese comic. In Japan he had lived out scenes from an early nineteenth-century

English novel. Life in Tokyo was like a pump room in Bath and life in London was like a game of SF porno pin-ball in Shinjuku. Something had gone wrong. It was Jane, of course. Around her, everything went wrong.

'Where were you?' he said about half an hour afterwards. She was wearing the crumpled hibiscus bathrobe and he had regained his boxer shorts.

'I was *here*, wasn't I?'

'You failed to answer the entryphone.'

'Yeah, well, they cut it off, didn't they?'

'Did they?'

'Yeah, or I wouldn't have *said* so, would I? Don't ask me *questions* all the time.'

'I was trying to discover who, whom, who cut off the entryphone. *Who* cut off the entryphone?'

'Council. They're trying to get me out, aren't they? Making aggravation. But I've still got my *certificate*, haven't I? So they can't actually sling me out, can they? So they try cutting things off, don't they? Like the entryphone. They switched it off on me.'

'Off on you?' Of course, thought Suzuki, even as he vocalised the repetition. Off on. English prepositions could go together in almost any combination. Up in my room. Come on in. What was that one he had learned watching the snooker on television? It's an in off. Once again Suzuki suffered a sudden, sharp attack of the fear that he would simply never make it with the English language: it was a corridor lined with doors, any one of which opened up on to – up on to! – an aircraft hangar packed to the roof with fresh difficulties. The attack passed, leaving this other fear,

74

the one induced by her. Now was the time to withdraw: to assemble his clothing, bow low, and go. He opened his mouth to speak, and found himself asking 'What magnitude of sum would be required to alleviate your immediate difficulties?'

'Eh?'

Suzuki said it again, this time stumbling slightly. He had no trouble remembering the sentence. It had been well rehearsed. But he was disconcerted to find that she did not immediately understand it. She got it the second time, however.

'Oh Sue, you *can't*. It'd be hundreds and *hundreds*.'

'I would be privileged to help you with your financial problem. Is that all the money you owe? Just hundreds?'

'*No*, don't be *silly*. The bank wants *thousands*. I should sue that bank. They're dead scared I'm going to sue them, actually. Or write an article about them. They're quite nervous about publicity because of South Africa. But with the council it's only a lousy couple of hundred quid. I've already *told* them they're getting it when the article gets published.'

'By a couple of hundred you mean two hundred.'

'No, three hundred. And fifty. Four hundred if you count what I never gave them last time. Which isn't rightfully theirs. Bastards.'

It was more, frighteningly more, than Suzuki had bargained for. Then again, it could never have been a bargain. For this madness, he would receive his reward in the distant future, and only if disaster failed to intervene. As he rose and crossed to where his jacket lay crumpled, with one arm dangling, on top of the bookcase where it had been thrown, he recalled how less than half a century before men had gone to their

75

deaths in just this manner, with one overpowering foretaste of heavenly beauty at the Yasukuni shrine, before they were taken away to their appointment with destiny.

'You will not want to count this in my presence,' said Suzuki, passing her the sealed, long white envelope. 'So let me tell you it contains two hundred and fifty pounds. Perhaps it will satisfy them for a while.'

A Japanese woman would have placed the envelope carefully before her where she knelt. She would have gazed at it with bowed head as she began the long process of acknowledging her mixed relief, gratitude and humiliation. Suzuki was delighted by his own shock when Jane tore the envelope open, fanned the cash and threw it in the air. It was falling on them like leaves shaken loose by an earthquake as she kissed him. Within seconds he was giving her the Arm of Steel, her favourite preliminary manoeuvre. Straddling his extended forearm with her back against the wall, her legs around his waist, she pumped with her hips like an Olympic rower. This was what he loved about her. She didn't breach etiquette: she obliterated the very concept of it. She set him free. She gave him danger. They fell on the bed. Somehow still clutching a ten pound note between her teeth, she did an ever more urgent, ever more frantic, ever more vocal version of her near crisis, her near fulfilment.

'Yes! Yes! Fuck me, you Jap bastard!'

The words she used were only half comprehensible to him but then they always were. Through his own ten pound note he replied in kind.

'Wa, sugoi! Kimochi ga ii! I-ku! I-KU!'

After the shrieking and ebb-tide gasps they lay half dozing.

76

Still palpitating, she said it was too much money. Pole-axed, he apologised that it was not enough. She said she had done nothing to deserve it. He said that she had already given him more than she could possibly imagine. She said she was confident that the money would be enough to make the council agree it was worth waiting for the rest. He said he was sure she was right. She said she could never pay him back. He was sure she was right about that, too, but did not say so.

'I'm *hungry*,' she announced, as if it was a discovery.

'Do you want to go out? I could take you to a Japanese restaurant.'

'That would be lovely. I was *in* one. In Japan. Not tonight, though. Because we want to do more of this, don't we? Only done it twice, haven't we? I'll make us some dinner here.'

'Shall we go shopping?' He was yawning as he said it. A deep yawn that stretched him on a frame of bliss, like a high bar flyer who has already won the competition and flies freely into his corkscrew dismount with no anxiety for the result.

'You're shagged, aren't you? You're just a clapped-out old Jap *stud*. I'll go down to the deli at Farringdon and get some things. You have a sleep. Snoozy Suzy, that's you.'

She flicked his limp penis in farewell and went about gathering up money. Heavy-lidded, his vision filmed with sleepy tears, he drank in her naked poses as she stooped and straightened. She was from the Floating World. She had taken him there, into the city that lives by night. He was already asleep before she had finished dressing. The slam of the door came to him in a dream.

SIX

S UZUKI WOKE gasping from a nightmare in which he had
been forced to give a lecture, in English, full of words like
'elm', 'pulp' and 'emblem'. The most unsettling feature of the
nightmare was that the lecture was given on board a World
War II British battleship being attacked by Japanese torpedo
bombers. He was not, however, a prisoner-of-war. He was a
visiting lecturer. Insouciant British officers in white summer
uniforms sat in rows laughing at his mistakes while he prayed
for one of the torpedoes to score a hit. Multiple pom-poms
pocked the sky. The uproar was deafening but unfortunately
his voice could be heard almost as clearly as the laughter. 'Obviously, reliable logistic estimates will bulk particularly large
in strategic importance,' he had been trying to say. The first
word had taken what seemed like twenty minutes and during
the second word he had woken breathless.

He must have slept for hours. The light in the room was
all artificial and stunningly bright. Outside the window it was
dark. Jane swayed drunkenly before him. She was leaning on
everything within reach. It took a long time for her story to
emerge. Apparently the man at the delicatessen had wanted

her to give him quite a lot of money before he would let her buy anything. She said that when she and the man at the deli had been having their love affair she had been allowed to take home any food items she felt like but now he was saying that she owed him for it. Anyway, she paid him off and bought some stuff and then she went off with him for a drink at the pub and then back to the back room of the shut-up shop but he *still* wouldn't give her the money back. Anyway, she had got the things to eat and there was something to drink, which she had bought at the classy bottle-shop where there was another man she knew who said she owed him money. No, he wasn't the owner, he was just a man she knew. While saying all this she was laying out the contents of her carrier bags on the kitchen table. There was a frighteningly large tub of what Suzuki knew to be quite a good grade of caviare. There was a tin of pressed quail, a packet of smoked salmon three feet long and an inch thick, artichokes, truffles, bottled olives, a stone jar of Stilton and, incongruously, a packet of crisps the size of a pillow. 'Something to drink' turned out to be two large bottles of vodka.

'It's to go with the caviare. We're going to be Russians. We're going to *celebrate*.'

'How much did it cost?'

'I'm a good shopper. I'm very clever. I'm a famously clever shopper. I can make a little bit look like a lot. I could always do that.'

'Show me how much is left.'

'Don't *look* at me like that. Don't come *on* at me. I can't *stand* it when people *stand* there *looking* at me like that.'

'Show me.' He slapped her. If he had hit her with his

79

stiffened fingertips she would have died off the spot. On the spot. As it was she merely collapsed on to one of the kitchen chairs, which made a splintering sound under her, not disintegrating but changing shape, so that she fell off it on to the floor. Before she got enough breath back to scream he had discovered that there was barely thirty pounds left.

He calmed her down by holding her. He held her tightly enough to give her the alternative of shutting up or choking. He still in his boxer shorts, she still dressed for her disastrous expedition, they lay on her bed in the dark. He could see now that their liaison would have to end. What he could not see was how he would be able to disengage without being involved in a catastrophe. She was threatening herself with death even as she lay in his arms. Despairingly he made love to her again.

SEVEN

HIS TWIN PASSIONS for Jane Austen and danger having led him to the point where he craved a bit less of
both, Suzuki instituted a new policy of being hard for her to
find. It was meant to be temporary, while he regrouped. Very
soon, however, he discovered the magnitude of the imbroglio
in which he had become involved. In the days when he had been
willing her to turn up, she never did. Now that he was praying
for a respite, she was omnipresent. Sometimes she appeared in
the bookshop so suddenly that he barely had time to dart into
the back room. Keiko and Mitsuko covered for him. They told
her that he had gone to the embassy, to Tokyo, to the moon.
At the end of the day he left by the back door, stepped across
the alley and into the kitchen of the Namida restaurant, from
whose front door he emerged shortly afterward, wearing dark
glasses and reading *The Grapes of Wrath*. In some ways, since she
was never off his mind for a moment, this was the most intense
phase of their relationship. The pattern of his life was altered
away from solitude. Safety lay in crowds. He spent more
evenings than usual eating and drinking with the Japanese
men of his own age group. Several of them were in banking and

finance. They talked grimly about an imminent collapse of the stock market. They advised him to turn his savings into cash. He laughed bitterly. Exercising temperance, drinking only one beer to their three, he still took a lot on board. Even in autumn it is always hot in those little Japanese restaurants that you can find on the side of Ludgate Hill between St Paul's and the river. Suzuki would arrive home on the last train to find his landlady complaining about numerous phone calls from the girl with the bad language.

With a heartbreaking expenditure of money and energy he arranged for a personal telephone to be installed in his room. To deal with the telephone engineers was like coping with Jane in the days when she had been hard to find. They never arrived when they said they would and always did when they said they wouldn't. By the time the telephone and its attendant answering machine were installed and functioning, he had missed hours of work and seen far too much of Mrs Thelwell. She had become possessive. One Saturday night he returned from a cultural event to find her sitting on his bed looking at a copy of *Bon Comic*. The cultural event had taken place at the National Theatre. It had been a play by a young British playwright about the decline of Britain. Suzuki had understood quite a lot of it, although when reading the programme during the first interval he had found it hard to credit that a young playwright could have been born so long ago. Perhaps irony was being employed. With these people it was often hard to tell. He could tell Mrs Thelwell was being ironic, but not from her voice.

'We can't be having this sort of thing, can we Mr Suzy? Look what he's doing to her there. Just look at it. Don't tell me what she's saying. That's her screaming, isn't it, these words here? You people are sick. Sick. *Sick*.'

It was her eyes that told him she was employing irony. They shone. She was more dressed than usual. Undressing her was a task, but he could see no way out of it. The smell of butter was strong. She said she wanted everything in the comic. Since the classified advertisements in the back featured every kind of vibrating device and artificial organ, it was obvious that she was being ironic again. She laughed quite a lot, when not sobbing. Clearly microbes and viruses were regarded as no serious threat. At one point the telephone rang. Without stopping what she was doing, or rather what was being done to her, she snatched up the receiver before the answering machine had time to click into action.

'Piss off, you bitch. He's busy.'

He was, too. He had never been busier. A new phase of his life began, in which he would come home after a hard day's work to find his labours had only commenced. Eventually he persuaded Mrs Thelwell not to wait in his room and throw scenes if he was late. But he could persuade her to this degree of forbearance only by promising that he would check in to her own quarters when he got home, no matter at what hour. He took to spending as much time with Rochester-*san* as Rochester-*san* wanted, instead of keeping to a strict schedule as of old. They drank Rochester-*san*'s excellent brandy by the quart. When Rochester-*san* made his usual lunge, Suzuki still dodged, but slowly enough to let Rochester-*san* live in hope that next time might be the time. If Suzuki stayed late enough, Rochester-*san* would send him home in a charge-account cab for which Suzuki did not have to pay. It was never wise, though, even at two o'clock in the morning, to omit tapping on Mrs Thelwell's door.

Suzuki entered an epoch of perpetual sleepiness. At the gymnasium he moved like a shadow. 'Wotcher, Akira. What's happened to your endurance? Been getting into one of our women? *Brrm brrm.*' It was Lionel, shouting under the shower. Suzuki, rinsing his head free of shampoo froth, smiled with his eyes closed. 'Bringer along to my flatwarming,' Lionel insisted as they dressed.

'Flatwarming? Yes. Excuse me. Could you say that once again slowly?'

'Housewarming. Friday week. New flat in Jamaica Dock. You can practically walk there from here. Unbelievable. So high up you can see Berlin nearly. I'll wry downer details, rye?'

Suzuki asked if he could go alone. Actually he would have liked to take Lilian along, but didn't know how to broach the idea. The beauty of her body had begun to preoccupy him. He wondered how this was possible at a time when he was sated with bodies. Jane's body, because it was accompanied by Jane's behaviour, he was now prepared to travel long distances in order to avoid. He craved her physical form, but with increasing panic. Mrs Thelwell's body, though of questionable texture and degree of freshness, was attractively proportioned but too available. Lilian's body maintained the pure condition of the ideal. One morning he was running on the treadmill when she arrived and prepared to run on the treadmill to the left of his. The treadmills faced a mirrored wall, so he was able to watch, as he ran, every detail of her preliminary leg-stretching exercises. Until then his eyes had

84

been occupied with the familiar gradations of the small sweat patch forming on his light blue T-shirt. For the first three thousand metres there would be no sweat patch at all. Then a dark point of sweat would appear over the heart. By four thousand metres it would have assumed the shape of a young fighting bull's face. Usually he ran for five thousand metres, by which time the dark sweat patch would be the shape of a teddy bear's head. On this occasion he had already seen the fighting bull's face begin to grow bear-like when Lilian showed up, looped her towel over the arm of her treadmill, and, before stepping on to it, went into a series of manoeuvres designed to relax the muscles and tendons of her legs. Staring fixedly into the mirror as he pounded along going nowhere, Suzuki studied the effects of tension on her long, satin-smooth inner thighs where they emerged from her apple-green silk running shorts. When Lilian stepped on to the treadmill, tapped away at the keyboard of its command system, and began running with a mile-eating gait that made Suzuki feel as short-legged as a dachshund, there was a chance to examine the effect of repetitive reciprocal arm action on her exquisitely positioned breasts. Her neatly pressed pink T-shirt had no wrinkles, but a set of temporary pleats radiated downwards and diagonally from each nipple as her stride alternated. Suzuki found himself being as scientifically objective about her shirt as he was about his. It was just that the objectivity was of a different intensity. Suzuki kept running long after his teddy bear had fully formed. He kept running until his whole shirt was dark. Only when she sent him a smile through the mirror did he press the button to slow down. Don't press the point. Don't push your luck. Don't push it. Don't push. Don't. Do not. Do. Not.

Not much later on he was alone. Lilian, her bare arms beaded sparsely with sweat drops that glistened like pearls on silk, had smiled goodbye and gone. Thinking himself unobserved, Suzuki was riffling through an elementary series of one-hand stands when he realised she was watching him from the gallery where the weight-lifting was done. She waved to him and mimed having a drink. She pointed to the clock and held up ten fingers twice. 'Her fingers are as long as my legs,' he thought. After a shorter version of his usual sauna he showered under cold water, thanking his ancestors that Lionel wasn't around. This meeting was going to be awkward enough without comment from the sidelines. He dressed with ceremonial care and headed for the bar.

Lilian could not have been more gracious. She was as clearly spoken as her navy blue business suit was well cut. She had a slim black leather attaché case with gold clasps and carried a beeper. 'The office always has to know where I am to within a few yards, day or night. Because of the different trading hours around the world. It's quite flattering, really.' Suzuki was impressed by her businesslike attitude. It turned out she even knew a few words of his language, from once having worked in the computer room of the Hilton hotel in Hong Kong. Now she was a stockbroker, but she didn't, she said, believe in flash cars and all that sort of thing. What she admired in men was forbearance and circumspection.

'You take good care of your body,' she said.

'You do not need to,' he said. He didn't risk saying 'don't'. In moments of stress it tended to come out as 'doughnut'.

'Do you have a girlfriend here?' she asked.

'No.' He said it with a lack of hesitation that surprised him.

Unfortunately she was not available to be his escort on the evening of Lionel's party but she agreed to come out with him on some subsequent evening later in the month, or early the following month. Suzuki rather got the impression that her time, at present, was not her own. He also, most agreeably, got the impression that she regretted this. She suggested that when the time came they might have dinner and go dancing afterwards.

As he escorted her up the hill towards the fork in the road which led to her office in one direction and his bookshop in the other, he was walking on air. Otherwise he would have noticed Jane sooner. She must have been trailing them from the gymnasium. Luckily she did not attempt a confrontation. Instead she was furtive. She hid behind things. She turned away and looked at window displays of shooting sticks, umbrellas and gentlemen's accessories. A tantrum would have been less conspicuous but undoubtedly more embarrassing. After the unsuspecting Lilian had stepped away with a well-controlled little wave, Jane was on to him like an interrogator. Suzuki, until Lilian was safely out of sight, pretended that Jane was a stranger asking him the time. It would have been more plausible if she had laughed less wildly.

'Well, *now* we *know*. Wanker. What a *wanker.*'

'Please? I don't understand the context.'

'Wan-KER. Can't do it. Can't take it. As soon as things get a little bit difficult you're off, aren't you? You're off out. As far as you're concerned, it's not on. Too much aggro. You're away.'

'Please . . .' The prepositions were bouncing like hailstones on a shaved lawn. Several passers-by, arrested by the volume

87

of her voice and her operatic range of gesture, had shown signs of stopping to listen. Luckily most of the people flowing around the unhappy couple were on their way to the office. Suzuki started to walk, doing the steering for both of them. She danced around in a semi-circle from left to right and right to left, talking at a high pitch directly into his face. It was an effective means of persuasion. Ready to concede anything, he promised to call, to call by, and – he didn't have to concede this, but found himself doing so – to take her to the warming of his friend Lionel's new flat. Over the Bank of England passed a JAL Boeing 747, bringing another load of alert young Japanese men to this fabled land of Dunhill cigarette lighters, Burberry coats, Waterford crystal and the Changing of the Guard. They had filled in their landing cards. They were looking down in anticipation even as he looked up in despair. Suzuki envied them the simplicity of their expectations. They didn't know what they were getting into.

EIGHT

S O THEIR AFFAIR began again. Suzuki realised that it
had never really stopped. The hiatus had been part of it,
a pause for contemplation, like that moment in the tea ceremony when the guest examines the cup, admiring its pattern
as a way of expressing gratitude. He and Jane Austen were
tied together like the two lovers in *Wuthering Heights*, except
that she was Heathcliff. He knew what 'wuthering' meant.
He could spell 'heights'. He was getting somewhere with the
English language. He was even getting somewhere with the
English people, especially the women. So why did he feel,
when the tube train pulled in, that it had come specifically
to run him over? Perhaps it was because he had discovered
the hidden cost of adventure, which is to alter the man who
wished for it, so that the expanded horizon is seen only by
someone else with the same name. Suzuki yearned for home
like a prisoner-of-war, fearful that it would find him changed.

On the next Saturday afternoon the Tate Gallery held
a most interesting cultural event. The collection of modern paintings had been rearranged according to some new
principle that Suzuki didn't quite grasp. To help ensure that

he would not grasp it, Jane insisted on accompanying him. This meant that they didn't get there until the event was almost over. Her mere presence was enough to reduce the whole experience to fragments. She kept telling him about painters she had known and about how she could have been a painter too. She assured him, in a series of piercing whispers, that every other woman present was a sexual deviant. Always eager, like any advanced language student, to eavesdrop on educated conversation, Suzuki resigned himself to hearing it in atomised form.

'Bloody disgrace,' said a bald man with long hair, 'picture as good as that Sickert hanging down there in the dark.'

'You sometimes wonder,' said the tweed-jacketed woman with him, 'why Stanley Spencer had to be quite so awful. Pitiless vision and all that, but why does he have to be *quite* so *awful*?'

'Why don't we ask her why *she's* so awful?' came the loud whisper in his ear. 'What a *dyke*! Ker-*runch*!'

'Can I help you?' asked the bald man. Suzuki, at a loss, bowed. A girl who could have been the sister of the girl in Whistler's portrait came running up, stopped near them, and called softly to a friend invisible beyond the archway into the next room. 'Pascale! Pascale!'

'Oo,' said the voice in Suzuki's ear, 'aren't we too tiddly-twee? I bet *we* pee *very* quietly.'

Actually Suzuki thought the girl in question was the very model of unpretentious refinement. Her shiny shoes, her patterned stockings, her silk and cashmere – if her hair had been straighter she could have been one of the fine young women of Tokyo. She might have lived in an Azabu apartment, with a living-room so big that you could walk all the way around the dining table without bumping into a chair. She would be a successful man's young wife, and yet she would have another existence, as a woman interested in cultural events. She would come to meet him in a coffee shop in Ochanomizu, near the bookshops of Jinbōchō. They would discuss some serious cultural subject. It would be a hopeless love. Of all its delectable qualities, the most cherished, for both of them, would be its virtual inaudibility.

'In a trance, are we? YOO-HOO! ARE YOU RECEIVING ME, JAPAN?'

As the first step in going home together to her place, Suzuki took Jane to one of the cheap Japanese restaurants near St Paul's. It was entertaining, in a way. Some of the young men present were acquaintances of his. They were obviously impressed. The low-quality *sake* made her drunk as soon as she inhaled its fumes. By the time she tried to drink it she could hardly sit upright. Her boasts about the perfection of her chop-stick technique proved to be ill-founded. An intact slice of raw tuna dropped from a considerable height into the sauce, splashing his tie. When he looked put out she restored his good humour by using her chop-sticks to tweak his nose. This could have been embarrassing but a group of acquaintances at the next table were open-mouthed. Suzuki was reminded of what a prize he had taken, or so it appeared. And wasn't the appearance, in such matters, the reality? *The look of the thing*. A useful phrase.

After he had paid the bill, with the additional charge for the broken *sake* bottle, it took all Suzuki's skill in the martial arts to get her from the table to the door. Luckily there was a cab passing as they emerged. The driver was initially hostile. At the end of the journey, the size of the tip Suzuki declared himself prepared to offer ensured that the driver would at least help to get her out of the cab. Suzuki alone, however, had to handle the task of getting her as far as the lift. By now she was dead weight. He employed a movement known as Moving the Bullock. Later, when he woke up in her bed, he felt a pain in his lower back, but it was probably because he was trapped under her. Later still, still feeling the twinge, after yet another hideously expensive cab ride he entered his own little room on tip toe, to find that all his silence on the stairs had been beside the point, because this time Mrs Thelwell had turned down the sheets on his bed only as a preliminary to getting into it. He was late. She was prepared to forgive him.

NINE

THE AUTUMNAL EQUINOX in late September is a national holiday in Japan. For Japanese abroad it is a time of long phone calls home and drinking parties to drown distance. Preferring to be alone yet still lonely, Suzuki gave himself a treat. The most important cultural event he had attended for some time, it was a new production of *Hamlet* by the Royal Shakespeare Company at the Barbican theatre. Suzuki was blessedly unaccompanied. Holding his expensive programme, he leaned forward alertly. He knew the work well, having studied the text in detail at school. Always painfully aware that very few of its phrases can be used in a modern conversation, he had nevertheless memorised them by the dozen. He could recite 'To be or not to be'. There was no line in the play he could not recognise. Now, however, seeing it acted, he continually found the words moving just too fast for him to follow. This induced depression, but it was a depression he understood. A confusion he did not understand was created by some of the action. When Polonius suggested to Claudius and Gertrude that he and they should withdraw to observe Hamlet, the conversation took place with Hamlet already approaching. If they could see him, why could he not see them? He was looking at a book, but surely the conspirators could not safely assume that he would not look up and see them. It was puzzling. After the performance, Suzuki – who no longer cared how late he got home to his own little room, even if he had to go by taxi – called on Rochester-*san* for a late evening drink and an exchange of views.

'Sheer bloody incompetence on the producer's part,' asserted Rochester-*san* with the carefully articulated crispness which proved that he had already been drinking by himself. 'Sheer bloody arrogance. Kind of thing that stopped me going to the theatre. Could have been a theatre critic. *Should* have been a music critic. Would have been right on top by now. Heard this?'

'No. Is it good? I have been told Rachmaninov is quite weak.'

'Don't you believe it. The *Preludes* are a big test of a piano player. Takes muscle, like Richter. But Ashkenazy gives them the punch *and* the lyricism. Listen to this.'

Suzuki listened to the extent that Rochester-*san* didn't talk. All over again Suzuki was fascinated by Rochester-*san*'s expenditure of effort. Obviously it mattered to him that Suzuki should hear this music. Yet he talked while it was being played. How was such confusion of mind possible? Unhappiness must be the reason. Yet he, Suzuki, who was unhappy too, would not do such a thing. Across the face of a sweet waterfall of notes, Rochester-*san*'s voice cut and hung like a helicopter.

'. . . *sad* that Brendel won't touch Rachmaninov. Got a real hate about Sergei, old Alfred. Told me about it once. Said he'd

94

rather do all the Bach and Beethoven and Mozart and Schubert and Liszt ten times each than touch even one little piece of Rachmaninov. Beneath contempt, he thinks. And yet when you think about it, Rachmaninov wasn't just a great composer for the piano. He was a great *player* of the piano. Like Brendel himself. Rachmaninov was *the* great player of Chopin. Better than Cortot. As good as Rubinstein. Well, *almost* as good as Rubinstein. Extraordinary that Brendel isn't impressed by that. Man who writes so well about music. I mean Brendel, not Rachmaninov. Brendel is a man who writes *really well* about music. *I* should have written about music. Would have been right on top, now. Chauffeured car, silver-topped cane, every column anticipated and dreaded. Anticipated. *Dreaded.* My paper did that for Ken Tynan. Could have done the same for me. Instead, early retirement beckons. I sit in those damned editorial meetings and I haven't got a thing to say. What do *I* know about the stock market?'

'It will collapse,' said Suzuki, his mind only half present. In his imagination, Jane sprawled wantonly and laughed. Mrs Thelwell suffocatingly warmed his bare back. Lilian rested one Reebok-clad foot waist high before her on the transverse bar of a Nautilus machine and reached forward to lay her chin on her shin, her breasts in her pink T-shirt divided snugly by her vibrant thigh. Suzuki had his confusions too. They just didn't show.

'What makes you think that? Listen to this bit.' Rochester-*san*'s finger traced the outline of a phrase recurring just where it was least expected and most satisfactory. It was clear that he felt such music as if it was something that had been taken away from him and given back too late. He was sadder than it was.

'Many Japanese men I know in the financial sector are saying that the American market is overstretched and must collapse very soon now. The British market also.'

'You see what I mean? *You're* telling *me*. And *I* should be telling *you*. I'm a thousand years older than you are and this is my country but you own more of it than I do. You lot even invented the machine this beautiful music's coming out of.'

'Not really.' Suzuki was very proud of his 'not really'. The 'l' was almost liquid.

'Course it is. National Panasonic. That's one of yours, isn't it?'

'Yes. A part of the Matsushita group. But Matsushita-*sensei* did not invent these machines. He perfected their use. Your video machine is in the VHS format, for example. Matsushita-*sensei* decided to prefer VHS above the Beta format. Sony had made the Betamax give the best pictures quality . . .'

'Picture quality.'

'Picture quality. Thank you. But Mr Matsushita said that the VHS was to be the favourite because it needed less maint . . . to maintain less.'

'Less maintenance.'

'Less maintenance. He was ninety-three years old when he made the decision. The Sony corporation did everything they could to talk him out of it. But he insisted that the customers came first.'

'You see? I never knew any of that. God, it's so *shaming*, being so bloody useless. Don't leave me alone. You always get up and go. Stay here tonight.'

Suzuki thought seriously of doing so. Rochester-*san* was

plainly incapable and even if he had not been would probably have been less trouble than the regrettable entanglement waiting in Suzuki's little room. But Suzuki could not contemplate a new day without a clean shirt. To buy one would cost him almost as much as the taxi he would have to get unless he hurried for the last tube. In these circumstances he could not let Rochester-*san* pay for a taxi. He caught the train with seconds to spare. Sitting ankle-deep in litter as the primitive device rattled and banged through its hole, he was overcome with Rochester-*san*'s sadness as if it were his own. He remembered what Hamlet said while holding in his hand the skull of Yorrick. 'Alas,' Suzuki quoted to himself, moving the tip of his tongue silently but correctly. Polonius hides behind the *arras* but Hamlet says *alas*. The two words sound different. Silently Suzuki practised. The point was not likely to come up in conversation, but you never knew.

TEN

L IONEL'S FLATWARMING had to be approached by means of the new Docklands Light Railway. Untypically for London, it worked. The flat was high up in a man-made cliff beside the river. Against his better judgment Suzuki had not tried to renege on his invitation to Jane. His trepidation soon gave way to relief. Though dressed like a homicidal maniac, she was oddly docile. She did not, for example, offer to drive the train, or engage their fellow passengers in a critical argument about its construction or their physical appearance. Instead she smiled sweetly and whispered in Suzuki's ear what she would like to do to him if they could only be alone. Suzuki had heard about some of it only in magazines.

Docklands was like the night-life area of old Tokyo except that there was no night-life. It was the Yoshiwara district with no-one in the streets, a Floating World with nothing on the water except gulls and the very occasional water-skier in a wet-suit. Arriving at the designated ziggurat, Suzuki and his escort walked halfway round the indoor ornamental lake whose central fountain, a giant inverted chandelier *cum* shower fitting, sent polychromatic coruscations of spray upwards into the atrium. Suzuki was pleased, if surprised, that Jane did not jump in. At the reception desk Suzuki sent up his name and was issued with a code number. After punching it into a control panel he and his companion rose in a glass capsule through spiderweb networks of metal struts until the atrium was all below them, the exultant central fitting on its floor looking like some deadly butterfly fish in search of a mate.

They entered a tunnel, still going up. Jane made a shape with her mouth which indicated, Suzuki eventually realised, that she wanted to be kissed. Suzuki kissed her with circumspection but she indicated that she wanted the full treatment, including the Arm of Steel. Crouching, Suzuki put his right hand between her leather-clad legs, reached up to hold the chromium-plated heavy-duty chain which served her as a belt, and lifted her so that the toes of her work boots were a foot off the floor. Grinding her whole weight ecstatically against his forearm, she licked his eyes before cramming his head between her breasts. Suzuki therefore missed the exact moment when the capsule arrived in the living-room of Lionel's flat to be greeted by a round of applause. There were at least fifty people cheering and whistling. Lionel greeted his latest guests with two glasses of champagne. 'Nice one, Akira, nice one. Endurance OK, then? *Brrm brrm.*'

Although all the exterior walls were glass, none of them slid, so Suzuki, even if he had wanted to, would have been unable to deal with his embarrassment by jumping to his death on the newly-built brick embankment far below. Nor was his embarrassment, he was surprised to find, as disabling as it ought to have been. Being with Jane was so intensely preoccupying in itself that it numbed him to awkward circumstances, even when, as was almost invariably true, she was the cause of them.

Meeting Jane Austen for the first time in his life, Lionel gave her a deep, searching kiss, which Suzuki was interested to see she returned as if it were simply a continuation of the embrace she had previously been sharing with himself. 'Ah, she'll fit right in here, Akira,' gasped Lionel upon surfacing. 'The main thrust is finance, but for some reason all the best birds inner field are sock-rollers.'

'Sock-rollers?'

'Make your socks roll up and down just lookin' Adam, doanay?'

Lionel's metaphor barely did justice to the truth. Though most of the men present looked like footballers and pugilists who had been loaned suits by Armani for one night only, every woman in the room seemed to have stepped from one of the advertising pages in *Vogue*, *Harpers & Queen* or (Suzuki's favourite) *Elle*. Suzuki's private filing system contained carefully preserved tear-sheets featuring such top-flight models as Paulina Porizkova, Marie Helvin, Jerry Hall and Yasmin Le Bon. Not many were admitted to the shrine, in which these high priestesses constantly swapped rank according to his fancy. His current favourite was Tatiana Patitz. Educating his eye for Western beauty had been a pleasure to him, but he had never expected to be offered, in the real world, such a plethora of stimuli as was now unfolded to him in Lionel's new flat. Before the performance at the Festival Hall; during the interval at Covent Garden; at many other cultural events he had seen beautiful Western women: but never in this concentration, undiluted by anything less. A basin-cropped brunette wearing not much except a broad Damascene belt and a black velvet T-shirt encrusted with silver leaves crossed her gold string sandals and through a smile of Michelle Pfeiffer-standard murmured '*Lionel*, he's *gorgeous*.'

'Sod off, foetus-features,' said Jane amiably.

'Ooh, and he's got an owner. Sorry darling, I didn't see the leash.'

'How would you like one of my Doc Martens up your snatch?' Jane added, smiling sweetly. Suzuki didn't quite catch the words but he was relieved that she was behaving so well.

'Akira, meet Francine Beckenbauer,' said Lionel. 'Francine plays in the margin for Duncan, Doenitz.' Lionel suddenly bent close to Suzuki's ear. 'Why don't you leave me to sort these two out? Go off and circulate, rye? There's Lilian over there. She's all agog.'

Suzuki knew what 'all agog' meant but didn't quite see how it could apply to him. Nevertheless he forged off through the crowd towards Lilian, who was decorating a huge leather sofa in which several of the well-dressed thuggish young men were camped as close to her as possible without falling on top of her into the surprisingly deep indentation caused by her lithe body. Suzuki, as he fought his way near, was faintly disturbed to find her body so familiar. Her ankles, for example, he knew in detail. He had realised already that the reason why she had not been free to go out with him this evening was that she was coming here anyway. But who had she come with? Perhaps she was spoken of by Lionel. Spoken to? Spoken *for*. 'What's your hurry?' asked a drowsy blonde who implausibly combined small breasts with a large cleavage. 'My friend Francine's trying to catch up with you. Don't blame her.'

'I wasn't,' said Suzuki.

'Keep moving, Akira,' said a hulking dandy Suzuki recognised from the gymnasium. 'They'll eat you alive. It's *sashimi* time.'

'The lovely Lilian's caught his eye,' said a girl in a basque and camiknickers. 'Score another one for Japan. It's the Pacific connection.'

'It's the Pacific Rim,' said the hulking dandy. 'Yum, Yum.'

'Stop dreaming,' said the drowsy blonde. 'She wouldn't look at you. She's got the *yen* yen.'

'She'd better lose it before Grecian Ern gets here,' said the hulking dandy, 'or the raw fish will be dead meat.'

But Suzuki, who wouldn't have understood much of this even if he had still been in earshot, had by now entered the orbit, or ambience, of Lilian. There was nothing between him and her except a final thicket of young men talking gibberish.

'Keep the Testarossa in the garage and drive the Cosworth Sierra all day, you're *still* coining it, mate.'

'Leave it out. You want the GT-40, same as Roger Daltry. Testarossa's a toy.'

'Countach's a toy. Testarossa's got more poke than *you* could ever use, no danger.'

'Never. Bird's motor.'

'Do me a favour.'

She cleared a space beside her by pinching one of the young men with discreet savagery through the expensive cloth covering his thigh. Suzuki's shame at the ordinariness of his clothes quickly evaporated in the evident warmth of her greeting.

'I should have realised this was where you were asking me to. How stupid of me. You're Lionel's friend, aren't you?'

'You are too?' asked Suzuki, getting to the point.

'Yes, but I'm here with someone else.'

'Which one is he?'

'He isn't here.'

'I'm sorry, my English isn't very good. Could you . . .'

'I mean I'm here with him, but he isn't here yet. He'll be along later. He's at a meeting.'

'It is very late for a meeting.'

'He's taking over a company.'

'A big company?'

'Small for him. Big in the financial world. It's a finance company called Duncan, Doenitz.'

'Ah, yes. Do the employees know?'

'Not yet. Some of them are here tonight. We'd better whisper.'

They had been whispering anyway. Smelling her perfumed breath in his ear, Suzuki felt wonderfully conspiratorial. To conspire really meant to breathe together: he had looked it up. In the distance, between people and small palm trees, he could see Lionel and Jane, both laughing. Francine Beckenbauer had joined the drowsy blonde, the hulking dandy and the girl dressed for bed. They were all looking in the direction of himself and his beautiful companion. Charles and Diana must feel like this, he thought: the, what was it? Cynosure of all eyes. He had looked 'cynosure' up, and then found that nobody who spoke English as a native language had ever done the same. It was one of their characteristics: they never used such words nor knew what they meant. Finding out what words they did use, and knowing what those meant, was what mattered.

'Come and see me,' said Lilian. Suzuki understood that all right.

'I would be more honoured than I . . .'

'Let's go over there near the window so I can give you the details without the whole world knowing. We haven't got much time.'

Lilian ascended from the couch with extraordinary lack of effort, thereby revealing that although her short inverted American Beauty rose of a skirt went all the way around her hips, her pale sea-green top seeded with pearls was mainly concerned with her breasts, stomach and upper arms. As Suzuki followed her lightly tanned bare back through the crowd, he noticed with gratified alarm that yet another glass of champagne had appeared in his hand. He could have sworn there had been an empty one there a few seconds ago. London appeared in front of him, running brilliantly into the far distance like a galaxy rolled flat. Lilian masked a portion of it with the shape of an angel. He was glad he had brought his Mont Blanc pen. It would have been shameful to write down her telephone number with an ordinary ball-point. He wondered if she had noticed his Rolex.

'If I stand close to you like this nobody can see what you're doing,' she breathed. His ear caught fire and flamed fiercely.

'When would be an appropriate time for this meeting?' he asked.

'Not before Friday week. Ern leaves for Brazil on . . . Christ, here he is. Just stay cool and keep talking.'

Suzuki could not remember the full name of the man who had just made such a universal disturbance merely by arriving, but he recognised the face from the covers of financial magazines and the business sections of newspapers. It was readily apparent why what the man thought of Lilian's immediate situation might matter crucially to anyone else involved. The two other men were obviously bodyguards. Fitting exactly into their large suits, they exuded physical authority. But the man between them had authority of a different kind. Even at this distance, across a room jammed with carefully schooled casual elegance, he exemplified accomplished calm. Though tanned and well preserved, he clearly didn't care about being well into middle age. His close-cut white hair would have looked thin had it been longer. Of average height, he was overweight and so conservatively tailored as to invite the random glance to slide off him. But there were no random glances turned towards him. Every eye was intent on his merest move. He was a cynosure, and not just for the young women but the young men. Emulation was in the air like desire.

'Do you know much about Ern?'

'I'm afraid not.'

'Don't worry. Nobody else does either. He's sort of my protector. It's perfectly harmless, honestly.'

Suzuki was told all about Sir Ernest Papadakis, apparently also known as Grecian Ern, while the man who bore these peculiar names worked his way at no great pace towards them through the throng, stopped every few inches by worshippers competing for his ear and eye. Suzuki vaguely wondered why Jane was not among them. Where was she? But he wondered harder why Lilian had considered offering him, Suzuki, her friendship, when by her own account she had nothing to give that did not belong to the man who was about to address them. Suzuki practised conversational openings to himself. *Good evening, I have met your lady friend only a few minutes ago and now I must leave for Japan.*

'And this must be the famous Mr Suzuki,' said the new arrival when he had finished lightly kissing Lilian's offered cheek.

'How do you do, Sir Ernest,' said Suzuki, alarmed to discover that his own name was already known.

'Our girl has told me all about you. She's a big fan of yours.'

'I find that hard to believe.' Suzuki was very proud of managing this sentence, so difficult for a Japanese, who, if he said such a thing in his own language, would be questioning his interlocutor's veracity.

'No, no, she's got a good eye for a sensible man, haven't you, love? Perhaps Mr Suzuki can look after you a bit while I'm out of town.'

'Oh, Ern,' cooed Lilian. 'People would talk.'

'*These* people certainly would,' said her mentor, 'but who gives a shit what *they* think? Especially the blokes. I've never met so many lemmings pretending to be lions. Flats, cars, boats and it's all a bubble. They'll be sleeping on each other's floors in a day or two. Make sure you go liquid, Suzuki.'

Suzuki felt that he already had. The two bodyguards were looking at him as if their eyes were storing the information digitally. It was a relief when Lionel came up, until he spoke.

'Where's that bird of yours, Akira?'

'I was under the impression that she was with you.'

'She got a bit jealous about all the attention you was getting and she said she was going to do something about it.'

'What did she say she was going to do?' said Suzuki, his mind suddenly as focused as it had been during his final examinations.

'Said she was going to kill herself, actually.'

'Did she say in what way?'

'Said she was going to jump off the building. Reason why I wasn't too worried. You can't jump off this building, rye? Not from the outside anyway.'

'Can you do it from the inside?'

'Well, yes, but . . . Shit.'

Suzuki beat Lionel to the lift but Lionel was the one who knew which button to press. The lift stopped just after it emerged from the tunnel and let them out on to a lattice-work metal gallery which ran around the top of the atrium. Its floor full of small square holes rattled as they ran halfway around the circumference to where Jane dangled from one of the jutting struts which were evidently intended to make the balustrade hard to climb over. Far below them, the poisoned fish fountain spouted rainbows from spikes which could have impaled a parachute regiment. Jane hung suspended from the strut by one or more of the larger links in the chain which formed her belt. If the belt had snapped she would not have fallen to her death. She was suspended on the inside of the balustrade, doubled up, hopelessly entangled and whining like a fox in a trap. As Suzuki and Lionel laboured to free her, she tried to form words through her sobs, but failed. Only when she was sitting down, with Suzuki cradling her head and shoulders against his chest, did her weeping find room for words.

'Oh Suzy, it's all gone wrong. Saul gone *wrong*.'

'It's all right,' said Suzuki over and over, feeling as guilty as if he had struck her. After a while Lionel said something about leaving them together, and left.

'I'm so fucked *up*. Snow *wonder* you don't want me.'

'I do.'

'You *don't*.'

'I do,' he lied, because at that moment he didn't. 'You are the most important . . .'

'It's all gone wrong and I can't fix it. I can't get *out*.'

'There, there.' Suzuki had got that one from Rochester-*san*: part of a lesson on the importance of the meaningless phrase. Suzuki was sad to notice that Jane had wet herself. On the other side of the circle the lift descended from its tunnel. Lilian, Sir Ernest and the two bodyguards were standing in it. They all looked across at him and Jane. Cynosures. Lilian lifted her hand in a little wave, perhaps meant as a promise, but taken by Suzuki to mean farewell.

ELEVEN

HE SOON CHANGED his mind about that. After all, Lilian had given him the go-ahead. As his new dictionary of English idioms explained, the go-ahead was not the same as the come-on, but it was still an invitation. On the day after Lionel's flatwarming party the stock market crashed. The day after that, Lionel asked Suzuki about the possibility of sleeping on his floor.

'I won't forget this, Akira,' said Lionel as he moved in. 'Always said you was a white man at heart.'

Big physically if not in spirit, Lionel, even with the few belongings which his creditors allowed him to retain, crowded the room to the point where Suzuki felt he might as well be back in Japan, but before the week was out Mrs Thelwell had transferred her attentions from her tenant to his new guest. Lionel took to spending most of his evenings in her part of the house, leaving Suzuki feeling more energetic than he had for some time. His relationship with Jane Austen had similarly ceased to be carnal. Regularly after his day at work, he called on her at her flat, where, with precedent-breaking reliability, she was always to be found at the appointed time.

It had been agreed between them that she would concentrate on her article, which would principally consist of an interview with Suzuki. When he came to call, her notebook would be open on the table. She would be holding a pen. She would switch on her tape-recorder and interview him.

'Um, what's your favourite colour, then?'

Suzuki was less worried by such questions than he might have been. They were the kind of questions that Japanese journalists always asked even in the most heavy intellectual magazines. The truth was that for the moment Suzuki wanted nothing from her except peace. He didn't care by what medicines her new-found tranquillity was being achieved. It was odd that she was allowed to give herself her own injections, but no doubt the famous National Health Service knew what it was doing. Suzuki's only thought was of how to disengage, and this would have been so even if a liaison with Lilian had not been in prospect.

'Are you sticking it into Miss Tiddlytits, then?'

Suzuki reached out to switch off the tape-recorder. 'No,' he said truthfully, because he hadn't as yet. He still found it hard to believe he ever would. Perhaps he would find out the day after tomorrow.

The next evening he called on Rochester-*san* for a scheduled mutual language lesson and found his host transfigured. Rochester-*san* was wearing a purple velvet lounging jacket. There were candles burning. Beyond and below the balcony, the long ornamental lake was already filling up with the reflections of the dormitory blocks, the Guildhall School of Music and Drama, and the strange theatrical complex in which Hamlet was unable to see Polonius, Claudius and Gertrude even when they had neglected to conceal themselves behind the arras. Alas.

'This one's a Krug. Hold your glass close while I pop the top. Nothing's too good for the Man from Japan.'

'You are very generous.'

'Least I can do. Still can't believe my luck. There I was at an editorial meeting with fuck-all to say and then when the financial editor was droning on about the economy I just said I'd been hearing from my Japanese contacts that a big market shift was just around the corner.'

'Did they listen?'

'Ah, that's where the deputy editor made his big mistake. Editor wasn't there, of course. Up in Sheffield watching a snooker tournament. But the deputy editor *and* the financial editor had a fine old time taking the piss out of these Japanese contacts of mine. Got the whole meeting falling about. So everybody remembered it. And when the market went zonk and we didn't predict it, the editor got to hear that I'd known in advance. Through my Japanese contacts, right? So now *I'm* going to be the deputy editor.'

'Congratulations.'

'*Omedote.* Is that what you say?'

'*Omedetō gozaimasu.*'

'You bet. Have another. Nothing's too good for my Japanese contacts.'

An opulent if indigestible catered meal having been sent in, they ate by candle light, with Chopin Nocturnes unspooling softly from the speakers in the crowded bookshelves.

'First thing I'm going to do as deputy editor,' said Rochester-*san* over a large brandy, 'is I'm going to publish that excellent little poem of yours on the book page. With a photograph.'

'I'm unworthy of such an honour.'

'Don't you believe it.'

Rochester-*san* tried to kiss him afterwards but Suzuki politely declined. Instead, they just danced.

TWELVE

IT WAS FRIDAY evening. Suzuki, despite everything, had
worked a hard week. But Lilian had forbidden him to go
home for a bathe and a change of clothes. 'You can do all that
here,' she said on the telephone. It sounded promising. His
spare shirt burning a hole in his briefcase, for the whole of
the entire, interminable tube ride to Sloane Square Suzuki
thought about the different ways things might go wrong. There
was scarcely room in his life for more disorder. Mrs Thelwell
was temporarily out of the way but how long would Jane lie
dormant? He had given her the last of his money. What had
she done with it? Certainly she hadn't eaten it. Except for the
occasional bunch of madly expensive out-of-season grapes she
never had any food anywhere in sight. Suzuki was shamefully
glad not to be seeing her that evening. Instead, he was seeing
Lilian. He had told Jane that he was scheduled to give a lecture
at the Japanese embassy, on the history of Kabuki. It was almost
true. In a week's time he *was* scheduled to be appearing at the
Japanese embassy, only the lecture on Kabuki would be delivered by a famous visiting Kabuki actor, with Suzuki functioning
merely as the interpreter. To handle the occasion competently,

however, would be an important step. Influential people would be watching. Mistakes would be remembered. He wished he did not feel the same about tonight.

Pink brick with white plaster trimmings, the many-windowed Victorian residential block was unnervingly massive. Her name beside the bell would have been frightening enough in itself. LILIAN PFLIMMLIN. Could even *they* pronounce a name like that? But her voice sounded warm through the crackle of the entryphone, and when the door of her apartment swung open the instantly apparent luxury of how she lived was comfortingly offset by her off-hand mode of dress.

'Tonight I'm your *geisha*,' she said after giving him a small kiss hello. 'So I thought I'd wear this. What's it called again?'

'A *yukata*.'

'*That's* it. The kimono's much more complicated, isn't it? Must take ages to get on and off.'

'Did Sir Ernest give you that?'

'I make quite a lot of money all by myself. And what I like about this is I can just walk around the place barefoot with nothing underneath. So all the gold thread just makes it look fancy.'

'I'm afraid to touch it.'

'Why don't I take it off, then?'

True to her word, she was naked underneath. He had rather suspected that she might be. This time she kissed him more thoroughly. He felt awkward.

'Don't you think,' she murmured, 'that you might put down your briefcase?'

He felt less awkward after that. She didn't smell of butter at all. In the bath they sat facing each other, with so much room to move that they didn't need to entwine their legs. They did anyway.

'I always wanted a huge bath, so I got this one built specially. Are you disgusted that I didn't have a shower before I got in?'

'No. I can't believe you ever need to.'

'I'm making you break *all* the rules, aren't I? Fancy a *geisha* just jumping on you like that.'

'Nowadays we call them *geiko*.'

'Have you ever had one?'

'On my salary? Not in a million years.'

Suzuki was very proud of this latter expression, which he had borrowed from a novel by the important modern English writer Penelope Mortimer. Sinking below the frothy surface, he blew a stream of water vertically through the suds, like a sperm whale in flummery. He emerged again to find her smiling. He smiled back. He was very happy. Not having conquered her yet, he felt as if he already had. No, better: as if he didn't need to. She was a dream that insisted on coming true, like her bathroom. Reflected from opulently framed mirrors, bent around the shoulders of treasurable bottles, he could see himself and his stellar princess, caught running away together, buried to their necks in cloud, waiting to be trampled by winged horses: an epic picture on ivory screens, flaking gold panels sliced by emerald leaves of young bamboo, decorated everywhere with the rubrics of an enchanted language: Ultra Glow, Teinte Creole, KISS MY FACE, Conquête du Soleil, KLORANE Shampooing Vacances, HAIR SO NEW Instant Detangling Cream Rinse – the eternal, unplumbable mystery of the West.

On her bed, which was itself larger in area than the room in which Suzuki had been brought up, Lilian lay in the half dark and lifted her arms to him. 'Just taste me for a little while, darling. Don't do the whole thing straightaway. Mustn't be a greedy guts. Start there.'

Suzuki started there.

'And now there.'

Suzuki moved to there.

'Now you do that while I do this.'

While she did this, Suzuki did that. He had never met such a figure of authority. Not even Shimura-*san* spoke with such quiet command.

'*God* you've got such a touch. Never again will I go *near* a man who eats with a knife and fork.'

Suzuki tasted his fingertips.

'Give me a taste too.'

Suzuki hadn't known that was allowed. *Bon Comic* had never mentioned it. Not even the correspondence section of the Japanese edition of *Penthouse* had ever hinted at such a thing. This girl loved herself.

'I think all sexy women must, don't you? If you weren't here to touch my nipples, *I* would. Like this. I'd be a fool not to, wouldn't I? When it feels so nice. Do you like watching that? Do you?'

He did.

'I could always make myself come like this, even before I had breasts to go with them.'

Suzuki, who had felt for some time that his general proportions had come to resemble those of a T-square, offered to enter her, but she made him wait.

'Have you been good? Have you been careful? Are you sure you won't give me anything but love?'

'Yes.'

She still made him wait until the critical moment, and then insisted that he advance only as quickly as she advanced in the opposite direction, taking him in by the gulp as her gasping mouth lifted to be kissed. Her hands were still caught between them when she locked her legs around his hips and mumbled: 'Don't you dare.'

'I'm sorry?'

'Don't you *dare*. Not yet. Stay there. Stay big. Think of something awful.'

'I don't understand.'

'Don't you think of something awful to stop yourself when you're trying not to?'

'Trying not to what?'

'To *come*, dope.'

'Oh yes. I have read about that. No, I have never done so. Perhaps I should try.'

Suzuki made a token attempt to think of something unpleasant but the circumstances were to the contrary. Although she made no move, she would have had to stop breathing. The enthralling mingled odours of her body would have had to dissipate. She would have had to vanish. Instead, she sighed, she gave a little quiver, and he let loose.

'I apologise.'

'Don't be a dope, you lovely man. You really are such a *dope*. I've thought about this all day. Now you stay right where you are for a while so it doesn't all come running out.' She sighed again, turned her head sideways, closed her eyes, pursed her lips, opened her eyes, looked into his face without turning her head, closed her eyes again, relaxed her pursed lips into a smile, snuggled her head deeper into the pillow, and hummed.

'What's that?'

'Just anything. Any happy tune.'

Later on they took a shower together, preparatory to going out for dinner. After the shower, however, she decided that it was necessary to go back to the bedroom. Suzuki was already getting used to the idea that she would be making all the decisions. Standing on his hands, he gazed into her lush spun-honey delta region as she knelt before him. He could feel her voice getting warmer. 'I watched you doing this for weeks before you realised it,' she said, 'and *I* always wanted to do *this*.' She was quite insistent that he maintain the pose. Finally he collapsed, though it was clear that she was the one who had been satisfied.

'I'm not so sure I need anything to eat after that.'

One of his own fantasies, however, was realised after the telephone rang. He had always wanted to be the silent lover in *Big Comic* who grazed voraciously while his powerful Western mistress was talking on the telephone to her black assassins, or in this case to her . . . to her what? (To her whom?) Her husband? Her real lover? The executor of her desires? His executioner?

'Princess Custard Slice?' asked the amplified voice of Sir Ernest Papadakis.

'Hello darling,' Lilian replied. 'Is it wonderful there?'

'Wonderful and dangerous. Is it the same there?'

'Sort of. Are you going to the *fazenda* tonight?'

'When the rain stops. You can't see the Sugar Loaf for blue cloud at the moment.'

'Who's driving? Robercico?'

'Yes, with João in the other car. Guns everywhere, don't worry.'

'Just don't stop for any roadblocks. Unless the men dressed as police are actually wearing shoes.'

'I miss you a lot. Especially at times like this.'

'You're always with me.'

Behind and below the conversation, Suzuki understood this last part and wondered how she could say it. But he resolved to do his real wondering next day, or next year. After she hung up she stroked his neck with both hands instead of one. Eventually there was a protracted shudder of some violence but small amplitude, so that he was able to follow it with his kiss. After his head joined hers on the pillow she was silent for some time before murmuring strangely: 'Why eat out when you can eat in?'

'I'm sorry?'

'Oh, don't be, Mr Suzuki. Don't you be sorry for a minute.'

Unconvincingly out of character, she pretended to let him help her choose a dress, rejecting all of his suggestions except the Donna Karan suit. Her wardrobe alone could have housed Suzuki's mother, sister and both aunts. Her car was parked nearby in the street.

'You'll have to forgive me for this boring little Targa,' she said, looking at him instead of the door lock while she turned the key. 'Ern likes me to keep a reasonably low profile when I'm out. He's right, of course.'

It was Suzuki's impression that they never stopped accelerating until she put on the brakes and they came sliding to a stop in front of a restaurant impossibly named Flaherty's.

'This place is a hideyhole nowadays,' she explained as they followed the head waiter through the genteel uproar to the only empty table. 'The man who ran it used to be famous but he tried to set fire to his house.'

'What happened?'

'He set fire to himself instead. Let's eat just a few *little* things.'

Suzuki took one look at the poster-sized menu and immediately became very worried about the bill. After his most recent subvention to Jane he had almost nothing left to his name except the homeward half of his return air ticket. But Lilian had an encouraging capacity to read his mind.

'This is on me, incidentally.'

'I couldn't allow that.'

'Don't argue. If you knew how much money I made you'd come running at me waving a little sword. Instead of doing the marvellous things you do.'

'Thank you.'

'Yum. Oysters. We could stay with the champagne to wash them down, couldn't we?'

Suzuki felt displaced, as if he were attending a cultural event but had not managed to obtain a printed programme. That man over there who was smoking a big cigar and looked like the actor Michael Caine: it *was* Michael Caine. It followed that the blindingly beautiful girl at the next table looked like Tatiana Patitz because she *was* Tatiana Patitz. In her own way, Lilian made even more happen than Jane did, but whereas everything Jane instigated was chaos, with Lilian it was all control. The life she led just looked fantastic. Then it made you afraid by proving actual. It was real. There was no escape. One couldn't just close the comic and pick up a text-book. The waiters kept bringing him more to cope with. Once again he seemed unable to keep his champagne glass empty.

'I think having a few little things *was* a better idea than having something big, don't you?' From inside her handbag her beeper beeped. 'Market must be closing in Chicago. Mind the fort for a bit while I find a phone. Later on we'll go dancing, yes?'

Only seconds after Lilian had vacated her seat, another woman had slid into it. This one was less fashionably dressed but seemed, if possible, even more confident.

'Val Butcher,' said the newcomer. 'I've been hearing a lot about you from my old friend Jane Austen. She says you're quite a goer.'

'I have not gone yet. Possibly I will stay here in London.'

'Witty, too. And you must be pretty brave, coming between Grecian Ern and his bit of fluff.'

'I'm sorry?'

'Well said. The whole City's talking about you after that pre-Crash bash down in Docklands. You must really have it where it counts. You've got the dolly-birds jumping out of windows.'

'I don't understand.'

'And Ted Rochester tells me you're the hottest Jap literary prospect since that mad poofter with the motorbike who cut the Emperor's head off, what was his name?'

'Mishima. I hardly deserve such . . .' Suzuki began, but

by that time Lilian had returned. The interloper delivered a farewell speech while rising and walking backwards.

'Just keeping him warm for you, Miss Pflimmlin. Not that he looks like you've been neglecting him, if I may make so bold . . .' These last words were addressed to the back of Lilian's neck.

'I should have known I couldn't take my eyes off you for a minute,' said Lilian, even as the retreating interference was still audible behind her. 'Not that I ever want to. What I want to see you do next is dance. I'll bet you can dance like mad.'

In the thunderous interior of a club called The Tempest Suzuki tried to show her she was not wrong. His carefully polished fox-trot, however, turned out not to be appropriate. The floor was jammed solid. The music was so loud that one beat joined to the next. Though volcanic flames flickered in the distance and thin shafts of light transgressed the infernally writhing gloom at unexpected angles, he could see almost nothing except her face, and then lost sight even of that as she clasped him tightly and shouted in his ear.

'. . . et's sit thi . . . one ou . . .'

'I'm sorry?'

'SIT THIS ONE OUT.'

'Yes.'

Two rooms away it was slightly less dark and marginally more quiet. A few decibels' difference made speech possible, and every few seconds you could see to whom you were talking. Bolts of photoflash emanated from a young Viking motor-cyclist holding a camera. In lounge chairs lounged young ladies of an imaginative elegance unknown even to Suzuki's filing system.

'You won't look at me now that you've seen this bunch,' said Lilian.

'Hello,' shouted Francine Beckenbauer, gliding near.

'Goodbye,' shouted Lilian, adding, in nearer normal tones: 'Ern should have screwed that girl. Then she'd have known her place.'

But Suzuki was looking at the full glass in his hand. Who had put it there? And what was he going to call his new mistress? Without being able to pronounce her name or any part of it, he had done things with her which defied memory. How could he ever go home? How could he not? What was Jane Austen doing at that moment?

'A Miss Jane Austen is here,' said a large black man in a blue suit. He was behind their couch, leaning down between them so they could both hear him. 'She's very banned here, but she says she's got a message for Prince Suzuki.'

'For Prince Suzuki?' asked Lilian, with a look of slight puzzlement that was enough to transform her.

'She says she's got vital information for the Emperor's son.' The man's breath smelled seriously of onions.

'Tell her,' said Lilian with a smile, 'to bugger off.'

Suzuki missed Lilian's smile because his gaze was focused on the dark space which must have been one of the entrances to the room. In a sudden lightning flash he had seen Jane struggling between two suited men even bigger than the one breathing in his ear. There was another lightning flash and he could see that her arm was being twisted. He knew how easily the urge to twist Jane's arm could arise even in the heart of a pacifist but there was something about the spectacle that made him feel the overwhelming importance of bringing it to an end. Threading his way quickly between chairs and couches, he reached the agitated group, grasped the upper arm of the man doing the twisting, and pinched.

'Oh Suzy,' wailed Jane, barely audible over the man's wounded screams, 'He was *hurting* me.'

The other man, stepping over his partner's writhing body, drew a short but heavy-looking stick from an inner pocket. Suzuki was hampered by Jane's full weight draped around his neck. He had no choice except to kick the man quite severely in the kneecap. As the second man fell down shrieking on top of the first, a third man, recognisable by his onion breath, arrived rapidly from behind. Jane had Suzuki's arms pinned so thoroughly that she might as well have been the man's accomplice. 'Leave him alone!' she screamed. 'He's a Japanese *prince!*' Suzuki took two very hard punches in the stomach before he was able to break free of her embrace and drop the black man with a firm but reasonably safe finger-tip jab under the heart.

By the time Suzuki had finished spitting out a mouthful of regurgitated oysters, two more men had arrived, both running fast. Suzuki saw Jane closing in again. There was no time to lose. Grasping one of the men by the lapels, he put his right foot in the man's stomach, fell backwards, and levered the man up and away into the dark, where his body made a splintering impact which indicated that he had fallen behind the bar. Still on the floor, Suzuki scythed his leg sideways and brought the other man down beside him. Unfortunately Jane was between them, still yelling 'Leave him *alone!*' Her voice stopped abruptly when the man hit her. Suzuki, angry for the first time, drove a stiff knuckle into the man's collarbone, which snapped like a rice cookie.

THIRTEEN

IN WEST END CENTRAL police station no charge was brought against Suzuki. 'You're a very lucky Oriental chap,' said the senior officer present. 'The old man of one of them birds you was with owns the place.'

'I am very grateful.'

'Oh, don't thank *me*, China. If it was down to me you'd be going home PDQ. Chop-chop in your language. Get me?'

'Japan. I am from Japan, not China.'

'Oh, I know *that*. You're a very clever Jap chap. Velly *crever*, in your language. Just let me tell you I don't like all these martial arts of yours one little bit. Never *saw* so much GBH. One of them blokes is breathing through a tube and the one you hit with the bottle needs his face sewn back on.'

'I did not hit him with the bottle. He hit the bottle by himself.'

'Yes, well *I'll* be hitting the bottle by *my*self if I have to deal with much more of this. You stay away from our girls. And especially from that blonde nutter with all the ironmongery in her ears. You aren't doing her a *bit* of good.'

Suzuki, knowing that the officer could not mean Lilian, thought of asking what had happened to her, but could not deal with the challenge of saying her name. A policewoman told him that Jane Austen had been taken to hospital. 'Don't worry too much about all that hard chat from the super,' she said while looking through some documents. 'It's watching "The Bill" that does it. They feel they sort of have to.'

Puzzled but grateful, Suzuki left. No police transport to the hospital having been on offer, Suzuki had to walk, and frequently got lost. It was almost dawn when he arrived, further frustrated to see the towers of the Barbican quite nearby. If he had known that the hospital was in this vicinity he could have steered a straighter course. Inside the casualty department he had to wait for almost an hour before being redirected to another hospital.

'She's in de-tox,' said a woman who must have been a nurse. 'Do you understand what that means?'

'A man struck her very hard and I am trying to find out if she was badly hurt.'

'Yes, well, she is in a pretty bad way, but not from that. She's evidently been taking a lot of stuff and now she's got to be stopped.'

'Will it cost a great deal?'

'No, love. In this country it's all on the rates. We get them fixed up so they can go out and muck themselves up again, don't we?'

The other hospital was in Hampstead, so at least it was near his home. He found her asleep, with a tube in her arm. Her skin, whiter even than usual, showed the veins within it like violets under snow. Drawing his chair close, he put his head gently beside hers on the pillow and in his own language asked for forgiveness. He told her he wanted her to live. He did not tell her that he also wanted to be free of her, although it was true. Unobserved, he was able to give way to emotion. The unfamiliar feeling of tears occurred.

After half an hour someone came to tell him that he wasn't allowed to sit there any more. By then he was composed. Bearing a cyclostyled schedule of visiting times, he walked the rest of the way home with comparatively little difficulty. On the underground he would have choked, and a cab would have cost more money than he had left in his pocket, or possibly in the world. He had lost track of his finances, as of life itself. All he knew was that his original idea of inviting just enough danger had been fundamentally flawed.

'I'd love to know who called,' said Lilian's voice. 'Leave a message after the beep.' He thought of telling the machine that she still had his briefcase, but she must have already known that. The only bright spot on Suzuki's horizon was that there was nothing left to go wrong. His whole world had caved in. He fell into his little bed and slept as if shot for the rest of the afternoon, the whole night, and far into the next morning.

Lionel woke him up. 'Wotcher, Akira. How's the endurance? Not that I need to ask. It's all inner papers.' Suzuki had been told by Lionel many times in the past that to keep abreast of all the national Sunday newspapers was the great secret for being able to read every level of the market. This was the first time, however, that Suzuki had seen Lionel and his research material together in one place. The papers were spread all over Mrs Thelwell's bed, in which Mrs Thelwell, wearing a stridently floral dressing-gown over her nightdress, sat upright among pillows, keenly reading the quality broadsheet of which Rochester-*san* was now the deputy editor.

'Look, you're even in this posh one. *Lovely* photograph. And *I* didn't know you wrote poetry. It's a *lovely* poem, Akira. *What* a surprise you are.'

Lionel held up one of the tabloids. 'This is my favourite. They caught you just when you was thumping this big spade, didn't they? Can't hardly see him, but Jesus *you* look dangerous.'

Suzuki surveyed with alarm a double page layout in which he could be seen variously embroiled with the security staff at the nightclub. JAP RAMBO GOES BANANAS said a headline so big it left little room for a story. It turned out that this was a strategic necessity, because there were few facts.

The Jap mystery man they are calling the Sushi Rambo bounced the bouncers in the wee small hours of Friday night at a Mayfair exclusive club. Called the Tempest, nobody knew how he got in. 'Suddenly he was tearing our £350 suits to pieces,' said top security operative Rod Koenig. 'It was totally unprovoked.'

'I personally have never seen anything like it, frankly,' said another security operative who refused to give his name. 'Now I know how they felt at Pearl Harbour.' Rumours that the Nip Nemesis may be the unacknowledged son of the Emperor were discounted next morning by officials at the Japanese Embassy. When shown our exclusive photograph, we were told: 'Very sorry, no comment.' All *we* can say is: 'Remember Hiroshima!' Britain has enough soccer hooligans of her own. We don't need to import any, least of all from the Land of the Rising Yen. Got it, Tokyo?

Suzuki reflected that in different circumstances his pleasure in having had his poem so prominently published would have been intense. Now he felt that it only helped to focus on him a beam of attention that would mean his doom. Undoubtedly the embassy staff would react by withdrawing his invitation to act as translator for the Kabuki evening. They might well impound his passport. For the first time in his life, Suzuki thought seriously of not turning up at work next day. He thought of doing what the British did, and pretending to be sick. It was too irresponsible a step. Not even the Americans did it. As if to confirm the rightness of his decision, a despatch rider delivered his briefcase. There was no accompanying message.

Suzuki arrived at the bookshop to be greeted by transparently satisfied smiles from the junior male members of the staff and looks of startled concern from the women, as if he had been struck by lightning and was standing there with smoke coming out of his shoes. The manager was nowhere to be seen, so it was Suzuki who had to deal with the telephone call from Val Butcher.

'Is your Mr Suzuki there, by any chance?'

'This is he. Speaking.'

'Oh, *hello* darling. Congratulations on the coverage, but I think we can do a bit better than that. I'm putting a little thing together myself and I need some follow-up.'

'Please . . .'

'Glad you're taking it that way. Listen love, would you mind telling me how many white women you've had?'

' "Had" in what way?'

'Christ, you really *are* a goer, aren't you? How do you feel after you've just poked one of our girls?'

'I can't talk.'

'No kidding? And then what do you do?'

'I'm afraid I have to say goodbye.'

Suzuki put the telephone down just as the manager came in from the street and headed towards his office at the back of the shop, beckoning for Suzuki to follow. The ensuing conversation was the most awkward Suzuki had ever endured. The manager, though speaking as indirectly as possible, clearly felt the same. Apparently he had spent most of the morning at the embassy, waiting to see the Cultural attaché, the *de facto* overseer of Suzuki's activities in London. Since Suzuki would one day outrank the manager, effectively the manager was delivering a message of admonition from one of his superiors to another. This put him in a desperately embarrassing position. He hinted that the Cultural attaché had been aware of this but so angry that he was determined to make others suffer too. The invitation to act as interpreter was not withdrawn. Indeed it was to be taken as an obligation. There must be no further anomalies. On the other hand, an early return to Japan was considered advisable, perhaps even before the New Year. Suzuki's position could be considered more carefully when he was out of the limelight. That Suzuki had ever got *into* the limelight – the Cultural attaché had made this brutally plain – must be at least partly the manager's responsibility. To send a prospective high-flyer abroad in order to learn smoothness, and then to find his face gazing out of the sort of newspaper which dedicated itself to fomenting international tension – well, perhaps the whole system would have to come under review. The manager had apparently not been offered tea. Suzuki had already noted that he himself had been denied the same courtesy. His web of supporting relationships was coming apart. That evening Jane still wasn't talking to him, but at least it was because she wasn't talking to anyone. For his professional acquaintances to deny him common courtesy, however, was a cumulative death sentence.

Next morning there were two more hammer blows. Having woken to the bleak prospect of the Kabuki lecture that evening, he packed his good suit, his new shoes and a spare shirt in his suit bag, along with his Tōdai tie, which presumably he would retain the right to wear even if he ended his life in gaol. Why did he presume that? They would probably hang him with it. As he left the house on tip-toe he was met by the postman, breaking all precedent by arriving early enough actually to deliver a letter to someone who had not already left for work. There was a special delivery letter from Shimura-*san*. The tube train, although half empty by Tokyo standards, was too crowded to allow for comfortable reading, but when it broke down between stations Suzuki, after the first half hour of immobility, found a way of retaining a grip on his briefcase and suit-bag while still managing to open the letter. If he had been sitting down it would have been easier. It would also have been easier to absorb the contents.

'I feel bound to say it was depressing', one part of the letter said, 'to telephone you at the number you gave, at a time of day less than convenient to myself, and be greeted by the words "Piss off, you bitch". I presume I have transcribed them correctly. Luckily I have only a vague idea of what they mean. Doubtless there is some explanation. But nothing can detract from the fact that your circumstances are not in your control. Was that the same woman as the one you told me about? Are there more? Not even the great Admiral Yamamoto, who had several emotional interests, would have been . . .'

The rest of the letter was in the same vein. Luckily it had been written before the night-club incident occurred, so at least there was no mention of that. Suzuki did not look forward to what Shimura-*san* would make of *that*. Shimura-*san*'s idea of spontaneous behaviour in public was the deportment of the Emperor Hirohito at his own funeral. Suzuki was shocked to find himself having such an idea. Was he becoming Westernised?

'Do you mind not poking me with that bloody bag?'

'I'm sorry.'

'Ear! You that Rambo feller what was inner paper?'

'Please . . .'

'Ear! Lorna! It's Rambo! The mad Jap!'

An hour late for work, Suzuki was beckoned straight into the manager's office and shown one of that morning's tabloid newspapers. It was the up-market tabloid, the one with headlines less than half the size of the page and a few items of cultural interest within. One of these articles featured a cropped version of the photograph of him hitting the black man. The black man was missing, leaving only Suzuki's contorted face and extended fist. There were also smaller portrait photographs of Jane Austen, Lilian Pflimmlin and Sir Ernest

Papadakis. The manager left Suzuki alone to read the article. This time, Suzuki noted in passing, he had been offered a drink – a large straight Scotch whisky. Perhaps the manager was becoming Westernised too. BRRM! BRRM! KARATE POET PACKS DOUBLE PUNCH, said the headline. THE VAL BUTCHER PROFILE. A small photograph of the author appeared under her byline. All in all, when the photographs were added together, there was not a great deal of room left on the page for prose. Suzuki soon wished there had been even less. After a brief introduction in which the few existing facts were garbled still further, the author brought to bear her powers of analysis.

At the Japanese Embassy in Piccadilly *tout Londres* will be there tonight. To see the sensational Mr Suzuki in yet another role. That of actor. In some extracts from the famed Japanese play, *Kabuki*. Ordinarily a big yawn, you might think. Yet suddenly the sinecure of all eyes – and for one reason.

So who is he, this talented, violent, violently attractive young man? That some of London's most hard-bitten reporters have so misleadingly called the Japanese Rambo? Because make no mistake: Rambo goes *there* to deal with *them*, whereas young Mr Suzuki comes *here* to deal with *us*. And by 'us' I don't just mean those oh-so-tough guys in the nightclubs of London's famed Soho, the Mecca for many a bus-load of Tokyo *touristi*.

Because there are also our women. And in Mr Suzuki's case they are the cream of the crop. The hardest to meet, the most expensive to entertain. Is it because he is the unacknowledged son of ex-Emperor Mishima, as some have rumoured?

Be that as it may, at least part of the Suzuki motor-cycle fortune seems to have found its way into the ready wallet of this wandering scion with the roving slant eye. If that's not a racist slur. And *I* wouldn't want to be around when Mr Suzuki was being sensitive to one of *those*. *Noh*-way!

Suzuki bit off an inch of Scotch and swallowed it whole. He was having a great deal of trouble following the thread of the article. Many of the sentences were without verbs, which made the syntax hard to unscramble. On top of that, the line of thought was so difficult to determine that he wondered whether the author herself would be able to paraphrase it.

Sorry fellows, but the sad fact is this. Mr Suzuki has got everything our girls want. He is a poet with the traditional Japanese sense of delicately balanced refinement which has been refined through thousands of years of their literary history where the emphasis has always been on balance and delicacy. And he can do it in English, too.

Which makes you wonder, will the English poem, like the English motor-cycle, go the way of all flesh? Will it once again be 'Oh yes, velly solly prease, our turn now?' That much is in the lap of the ancestors, as they say in Japan.

But the amazing Mr Suzuki isn't just a poet, he's a man. One who isn't afraid to be physical. Physical in both sentences of the word. His favourite colour, I am able to reveal, is red. Blood red: the red that flowed from the injured lips of those oh-so-tough guys in that hard-bitten nightclub.

And also, I can exclusively disclose, from another gang of local boys who resented his success with rising pop star Jane Austen, now in hospital. The same rising pop star who later had to be stopped from a suicide jump by Mr Suzuki himself at a wild yuppie party in a Docklands penthouse. That ended only when the stock market crashed around their ears. And who walked away smiling? Take another bow, Mr Suzuki!

Suzuki took another drink, leaving one more in the glass. He wondered if it would be enough.

But now the story takes off like a meteor. Because who should next fall for the poetic, whirlwind charms of our oriental enigma but stockbroker and beauty-about-town Lilian Pflimmlin, until then the only apple in the shrewd eye of pathologically publicity-shy international mega-mogul Sir Ernest 'Grecian Ern' Papadakis? Whose Australian passport comes by way of Athens, his untold millions by routes too devious to unravel?

Yet not even all the awesome power of the man they used to call the Adonis from Adelaide could hold Mr Suzuki back when he took one look at the delicious Lilian. I was there and I heard what he said: 'I'm sorry'. As if fate ruled the roost.

After the night-club wrecking incident that was called Hiroshima all over again by those who survived the sudden unprovoked wrath of her definitely not inscrutable admirer, *la* Pflimmlin has been unavailable for comment. But her close friend and fellow yuppie-ette Francine Beckenbauer told me exclusively: 'It was the blowfish lying down with the lamb. Something was bound to explode.'

Suzuki drained the last of the Scotch. He would have to go through the rest of this operation without anaesthetic. How had it come to this? When did it begin?

Getting an interview from Mr Suzuki himself is practically impossible. Not because he doesn't speak English as well as you or I – he does. But because he clearly believes that a good strong dose of Oriental mystery is the strongest card in that well-cut suit of his. So he says: *'Noh!'* Every reporter on the cultural beat has tried and failed.

Luckily I knew the ropes. Above all I knew the people. Following a web of contacts, I tracked him down in an exclusive Mayfair eating-club for the Jet Set where if they don't know you on the door, it's goodbye. But for me it was 'Hello, Val.'

And there he was, ready to reveal all. The lovely *Fräulein* Pflimmlin, in close attendance, discreetly absented herself while I asked her fascinating escort the 64,000 *yen* question: How many of our London ladies had he made love to? And he gave me an answer worthy of my old friend Warren Beatty.

'In what way?' he said. And there was a twinkle in his eye that I think he hoped was loveable. Perhaps it was. Perhaps I, too, was falling for the magic of this karate poet

who is at least no wimp. Then I asked him: And how do you feel afterwards?

'*I can't talk*,' he said. And suddenly I saw his tenderness. But then I asked him how he brought his evenings of love to an end. And he told me.

'*I'm afraid I have to say goodbye.*'

And then I saw his ruthlessness. I'm afraid I felt sick, Mr Suzuki. And I had to say goodbye, too. But I can't deny that I did it with regret. Perhaps yet another moth had come too close to the flame.

Apparently they've called him home. There's going to be some harsh words from the old man at the motorbike factory. But I predict there will be women hanging from the wheels of his plane like one of those helicopters leaving Vietnam, remember? So with singed wings I can only ask this. Will there be more like him, this T.S. Eliot from Tokyo?

Suzuki wondered if these last lines were quite in the right order. He stopped wondering when the manager rejoined him to say that a couple of journalists had already called that morning and been made to go away only after having been given the false information that he, Suzuki, would not be reporting for work. Suzuki got the idea that it would be better all round if this false information could be made true. Using the back door of the shop and the route through the restaurant, Suzuki was outside on Ludgate Hill before he realised that he had brought his briefcase and suit-bag with him. To go home to his room was no more advisable than to stay where he was. The gymnasium would be another bad idea. It was hours too early to go to the embassy, which would no doubt also be a target of press attention. Where could he conceal himself? He remembered a useful English expression Rochester-*san* had taught him: the best place to hide a book is in a library. Out of St Paul's Cathedral came a large party of Japanese tourists. They all climbed into a London Sightseeing Bus. Suzuki climbed in with them. Having found a spare seat on the open upper deck, he put his briefcase between his calves, draped his suit-bag over his lap, and explained to his companion – a man with prominently filled teeth in the old style – that there had been a mix-up. There was no untruth in that.

FOURTEEN

IT WAS TOO EARLY for the public to turn up. Judging from their uncultured appearance, the people waiting outside the embassy must have been reporters. One of them was eating, from a cardboard box, something called an Individual Fruit Pie. Luckily Suzuki knew an alternative way in, through the visa section. One of his monthly dining companions was on duty there. He greeted Suzuki with the restrained joy of the pregnant wife of a nuclear power plant worker after his escape from a decontamination unit. But the back-door route was made clear for Suzuki's unobtrusive introduction into the backstage area of the grand reception room in which the Kabuki lecture would take place. Suzuki met the actor, once a protégé of the great Yutaemon. The actor, whose stage name was Maruichi, was quite prominent in his field and Suzuki was able to ask for an autograph without hypocrisy. It was a bit like meeting a Sumo wrestler of the second rank. The actor had never quite made it to the top flight. Hence his availability abroad. While his contemporaries had been working every night at the main Kabuki theatre near the Ginza 4-*chome* crossing, this actor had been pretty well permanently on tour, spreading the message of his subtle art to the world. Subtlety he certainly had. He was a wonderfully accomplished performer. For the all-important *onnagata*, or female, roles, however, he had always been that crucial degree short of beauty, and nowadays he was also short of youth. He showed no sign of embarrassment about these facts. While Suzuki equipped himself with fresh outer garments, the actor talked freely about everything – except, mercifully, Suzuki's own adventures. To the actor, Suzuki was anonymous. It made a change.

Maruichi planned to do all the acting himself, except for one scene in which he would need Suzuki's assistance. It was a famous scene from the old play in which a great courtesan, the most expensive flower of the Yoshiwara district, casts a single glance on a visiting peasant and thereby enslaves him. The peasant's open-mouthed reaction to the beauty's searing glance presages his eventual ruin. The actor made it clear that it would not be necessary for Suzuki to register this reaction in any more than a token way. A mere lowering of the eyelids for a few seconds would do. Suzuki lowered his eyelids for a few seconds in the prescribed manner. When he opened them again he found that the actor had been joined by the Cultural attaché, who announced that the house was already full, with the press almost outnumbering the public. The press had been asked to occupy the chairs at the back of the room. There was even a television crew, from the prestigious BBC Arts programme *Kafka Before Breakfast*. While saying all this the Cultural attaché was gazing significantly at Suzuki, as if he needed reminding not to raise the possibility that these media attentions could be dedicated to anyone except the actor. While the actor and his dresser attended to the costumes, the Cultural attaché took Suzuki discreetly aside and advised him to enter the room at the same time as the actor, so that any additional stir that might be created could not be traced too blatantly to its possible source. If Suzuki had not already known that this meant him, the Cultural attaché's deep sigh would have been a broad hint.

The stratagem worked. Above the routine applause there was a vivid buzz of interest when they entered the unexpected warmth of the overcrowded salon, but the actor could have been forgiven for thinking that it was all for him and his first costume. He was dressed as a Samurai who had become a ghost, retaining his full armour, including horned helmet and two swords. The actor gave an outline of the story in Japanese. Flash-bulbs popped. The actor would perhaps have found it strange that the TV camera at the back of the room was focused on Suzuki. But the actor had his eyes closed, concentrating. Then he drew both of his swords and did a stamping dance, which culminated in a sudden rush down the central aisle, the swords whirling only just over the heads of the audience. When he reached the press seats the actor went into a particular frenzy, the swords whirling so fast that they looked like glittering wheels. Fragments of an Individual Fruit Pie flew through the air. Suzuki saw Val Butcher duck for cover.

Making up and changing costume in full view of the audience, the actor explained how the *maquillage* and full dress kimono of the Heian era courtesan were applied, assembled and secured. Suzuki translated. At school he had been obliged to learn the name of every piece of cloth involved in every variety of court dress from the earliest historical time until the modern age, so the task of translation, instead of impossible, was merely difficult. When he forgot the word 'gusset' he searched the front seats for a helpful female face. Neither Jane nor Lilian, of course, was present. But there were plenty of kindly looking Anglo-Saxon faces willing to help. He felt strangely close to them. On the other hand he felt strangely distant from the traditional culture with whose tensions and conventions his mind was so thoroughly stocked. Kabuki and Noh – what was their drama compared to the spectacle of a pale girl dangling from a balcony, of a goddess rising naked from the bubbles? What was a long evening with *geiko* and the few, sparse, plucked notes of the *shamisen*, compared with the splendour of these untamed women flickering in the thunder, mouthing incomprehensible charms like lovely witches, fighting for his damned soul? How could he go back to that old order, whose inexorable, suffocating tact the actor now proceeded to incarnate with a virtuoso twenty-five-minute impersonation of a certain noble lady of the court contemplating the vicissitudes of her forbidden love for a Muromachi Emperor's senior inspector of fortifications?

While the actor, accompanied by taped music consisting mainly of hiss and crackle, pursed his painted lips significantly or opened a fan with untoward abruptness in order to indicate a troubled spirit, Suzuki sat at the side of the stage area on his own specially supplied chair. From that angle he could see that Mrs Thelwell and Lionel were sitting near the middle of the room and to one side. Lionel held up an approving thumb and Mrs Thelwell waved. It occurred to Suzuki that he knew this woman far more intimately than his mother, his sister or either of his aunts. He scarcely knew her at all, of course – but then, the same applied to them. And with them he had spent a lifetime. Not a very long lifetime, but already he was getting towards being a third of the way through it, or perhaps more. Practically everything that had ever happened to him had happened to him here, within a few miles of where he was now sitting, with his legs crossed in front of him instead of folded underneath. Was there no other way of evaluating this turbulent present, except as the certain ruination of his future? Not that he could think of, no. Though his face did not betray it, fear returned to his heart, fanned by the realisation that the two men in dark glasses sitting in the row behind Mrs Thelwell and Lionel were the bodyguards of Sir Ernest Papadakis.

With Suzuki translating, the actor talked the audience through another costume change and readjustment of his make-up. This time he was turning himself into the famous courtesan of the Yoshiwara district. The women in the audience were particularly appreciative when he climbed onto his clogs and demonstrated the intricacies of the courtesan's special walk, with one clog swaying outwards in an arc before being placed carefully in front of the other, the whole demanding manoeuvre advancing in an unbroken flow. The actor explained that to accomplish this walk, while facially conveying all the subtlety of the courtesan's portentous interior debate about whether or not to place her spell on the unpolished visitor from a more pure world, was the great challenge of the *onnagata* actor's career, and one which he himself never undertook without first mentally rededicating himself to his art.

Finally the music started. The actor, with infinite slowness, began the long journey that would take him diagonally across the stage towards the fateful point of decision. Suzuki, in the role of the country bumpkin, stood patiently waiting to be glanced at. When, after an epoch had passed, he finally was, he was careful not to exceed his instructions, merely lowering his eyelids as he had been told.

Applause woke him up. He was being helped to his feet by two women. One of them he recognised by her buttery odour as Mrs Thelwell. But who was the other one, who smelled so strongly of talcum and eau-de-Cologne?

'Christ, what drama!' bellowed Val Butcher. 'What *drama*! You were *terrific*.'

Suzuki could see the actor, still high up on his clogs, looking down in what might have been either anger or compassion – the white make-up made it hard to tell. The Cultural attaché's emotions were easier to interpret. He was mopping his face with a Burberry handkerchief. It *was* hot. Perhaps that was why Suzuki had fainted. Anyway, that was the story the Cultural attaché was telling.

'Our young friend has been temporarily overcome by the heat and his responsibilities. But I think he is ready to continue with the rest of the programme, in which Maruichi-*sensei* will answer any questions that members of the audience might have about the art and history of Kabuki.'

'Just before that,' came a loud voice from the end of the room, 'just before that, if you don't mind, I wonder if we could be terrifically rude and ask for something we need?'

'I'm afraid I . . .' the Cultural attaché began.

'Wladislaw Januloviczesceu of *Kafka Before Breakfast*,' shouted the voice again. 'Could we just ask Mr Suzuki to do his wonderful stunned fall again? We just want to get another angle on it.'

'I'm afraid we must continue with the programme as planned,' said the Cultural attaché, directing this answer at Suzuki, who got the idea that his life depended on calling for the first question immediately. Luckily it was from one of the well-preserved women in the front seats. She asked a safely straightforward question about how a ceremonial kimono could be cleaned. Suzuki translated. The actor indicated every seam that needed to be undone and explained the individual method by which each had to be restitched afterwards. By the time Suzuki had translated all this the evening had regained the desirable stately pace from which it had been diverted by his fainting fit. He even had time to wonder what had caused it. Had it really been fear? Or had that moment, famous in the cultural history of his country, merely compressed into an instant the transfiguring extent to which he had indeed been stricken by the possibilities of a richer, wider world? Strangely he felt serene. The worst had happened. He was a dead man. Yet he was still breathing. Val Butcher had her hand up, trying to ask a question. Suzuki ignored her and chose someone else. Every press person wanted to ask a question but he ignored them all. The actor, Suzuki was glad to note, seemed happy to keep things as unchallenging as possible. The evening crawled towards its scheduled end. The TV camera lens had drooped. 'I've enjoyed this evening,' said a florid man who looked as if he might once have been an army officer. 'Especially that bit where you fell down. But I wonder if we really understand each other better after an evening like this. Each other's cultures, I mean. Do we *really* understand each other any better than when we were shooting at each other? Could you ask Mr Maruichi all that? Sorry I haven't been too concise.'

Suzuki translated, expecting an anodyne reply. This was touchy territory. It didn't do to be too specific.

'This is a good question,' said the actor to Suzuki. 'Perhaps you will translate my answer a portion at a time. It will give me time to think.'

'Of course.'

'My opinion is only that of an artist, not a politician, but after more than thirty years of constant travel all over the world, much of it in the West, it occurs to me that whether our cultures understand each other is not a meaningful question unless each culture understands itself. And here you have the advantage of us.'

Suzuki translated with a sudden sense of responsibility. This was going to be more difficult, and more important, than he had expected.

'No culture understands its own origins better than ours does. All of us Japanese, without exception, know better than you do how the country we live in came to be. But the *recent* past is a blank. Too many of us know too little about it, and we are not well served by those whose job it is, or should be, to tell us.'

Suzuki translated. The members of the press, he noticed, were all talking to one another. The TV man with the long name was talking animatedly to his cameraman. Val Butcher had a compact open and was repainting her lips. The public, however, was listening politely.

'Militarism was the great disaster of our country's recent

history. Travelling in the Pacific area especially, I have seen the scars of it, how long they last. No, not just scars: unhealed wounds, still festering. Yet our young people are not told about these things. Our media write silly articles and make silly programmes in countries we once damaged. Our silly television stars hold themselves superior to people whose parents suffered at our hands. We have raised a generation of young people who are brilliant at examinations but who know nothing.'

Suzuki felt as if he had been chosen for this moment. The actor had used the word *masukomi*, a Japanese contraction for 'mass communications'. Suzuki had known that this word needed to be translated as 'media'. English might be impossible to master but a little was better than none.

'Personally I hope that young people like Mr Suzuki – please translate this also – will leave the traditional arts to look after themselves and devote their gifts to the business of making popular entertainment more intelligent. There will always be Kabuki actors and master swordsmiths. What we need is more journalists and television announcers and entertainers who know what our country has lived through and can talk about it without arrogance and without fear. That is my hope for our country. And of one thing I am absolutely sure. Those of our young people who have dedicated themselves to learning your language and studying your history and your culture will play a crucial part in illuminating ours. Sometimes they become confused, caught between two worlds.' Here the actor smiled at Suzuki – a man's smile behind a woman's mouth. 'But the only future world worth living in belongs to them.'

The Cultural attaché was shaking his head at Suzuki. Obviously he meant that there should be no more questions. Whether he also meant that he had lost all faith in existence was harder to determine. It might have been the heat that had made him so pale. On behalf of the actor, Suzuki thanked the audience. Suddenly the television crew was all business. Suzuki saw the man with the long name waving at him. But when Sir Ernest's two bodyguards talked to the man with the long name he stopped waving. Then the bodyguards converged on Suzuki.

'Sir Ernest', said the merely big one, 'suggested you might like to come on over for a talk.'

'No offence,' said the really big one. 'We've heard what you're like in a punch-up. But it might be better all round if we went straight there without the press buzzing about. Nuff said?'

They had already led him up the aisle and were steering him towards a side room through the dispersing crowd. Some press men who looked as if they might close in thought better of it. 'Who are the minders, then?' one of them piped bravely, but from a safe distance. Val Butcher stood facing the TV camera, talking to the man with the long name, who was standing beside it. 'And then he was lying in my arms,' Suzuki heard her say, 'and it was a moment I'll never . . .'

Outside there was a big black Mercedes waiting.

FIFTEEN

SUZUKI SAT in the back seat between the two bodyguards. There was so much room that he did not need to make contact with them. He was surprised to notice his briefcase and suit-bag on the floor beyond their outstretched feet. How had that been managed? Far in front of them sat the driver among lights and instruments. There was no sound. The floodlit Houses of Parliament went past on the left. The floodlit Tate Gallery went past on the right. Suzuki had been to all these landmarks and centres of historical interest. But he had not been inside the new tower that rose beside the river. It rose so high that when Suzuki looked East through one of the glass walls of Sir Ernest Papadakis's penthouse he could see the fabulous historic *son et lumière* of the London night all the way to the Thames Barrier.

'Bit flash, I suppose,' said Sir Ernest. 'But I think it's important to be able to look down on Jeffrey Archer. That's his place over there. Practically ground level, wouldn't you say?'

Except for its acreage of window space, Sir Ernest's penthouse looked in no way modern. They could have been in

Kenwood House, waiting for a concert to begin. There was a plaster ceiling, of the type based on a design by the architect Adam, whose work Suzuki had come to admire extravagantly. He had clippings on the subject in his filing system. What would happen to his clippings? How would he get them home?

'I've got nothing against Japanese buying property in Australia,' said Sir Ernest around a large cigar. 'Your money is at least as good as ours. But *I* can't buy property in Tokyo.'

'Because it is too expensive?' Suzuki was having difficulty with his own cigar.

'Because there's a law against it. If you want smoke to come out of that thing you have to suck.'

'Yes. It is unfortunate. But Japan is very crowded already.'

'Japan is very clever already, but let that pass. When I do business in Tokyo I need a discreet little place to stay. Not a hotel. Just a quiet little apartment, like this one.'

'Yes.'

'But I can't own it in my own name.'

'No.'

'So I want you to take home about half a million in cash and buy some little place in the middle of town. Somewhere you'll enjoy, because I'll only be there about ten days a year. *You'll* be there all the time. Your cigar's gone out.'

'You are going to trust me with the spending of half a million dollars?'

'Don't be a dumb-cluck. Half a million *pounds*. We're going to need something with its own toilet. And when young Lilian prances through you don't see her sleeping on a futon, do you? Or perhaps you already have. I suppose you've seen her at every angle.'

151

'You don't mind about that?'

'I doughnut what?'

'Mind.'

'I mind intensely, my friend. But a man of my age who wants to keep a woman like that has to know when to let her go. Not that it hurts to get you out of the road for a while. Have you got a ticket home?'

'Yes.'

'I don't expect it's first class.'

'Economy.'

'Jesus. I suppose you *were* sent to Earth to remind me of when I was young, but I can't remember ever being *that* poor. My office will be in touch. OK *desu ka*?'

'You speak our language?'

'Only a few words. But I'm betting you speak mine. The boys will see you home.'

SIXTEEN

ROCHESTER-*san*'s new office was on the top floor of a post-modern building on the other side of the river. His old office, apparently, had been a broom-cupboard with a view of the incinerator. This one was so vast that his newly promoted personal effects looked lost in it. Outside, cold daylight sparkled on the long sweep of spires and blocks, domes and cubes, bulbs and stacks. Suzuki had come to say goodbye.

'Wonderful view, isn't it?' asked Rochester-*san* with satisfaction, waving his drink expansively. 'You can see everything. Jeffrey Archer lives just over there.'

'Mind that you continue with your studies.'

'You can just say "mind you continue". That "that" sounds intrusive. Tricky one, isn't it? Tricky language, ours.'

'Yes. It certainly is.'

'I'm *terribly* sorry I couldn't be at your lecture thing. Big dinner at the BBC. I was sitting next to Lady Susan Hussey herself. She's the Queen's lady-in-waiting, you know, as well as being Duke's wife.'

'How interesting.'

'Watch out for *that* one. People say it when they're bored.'

'Are you really allowed to say just "Duke" instead of "the Duke"?'

'It's his nickname. Like Duke Ellington. You'll *never* get that stuff right. The Americans can't either. Forget it. I should just forge on. You've done very well.'

'Oh, I don't know.'

'Boy, you're *famous*. That new piece by Val Butcher: she's in *love*. And the stuff on television when you passed out! They've been running it on CNN.'

'I must go. Alas.'

'Good time to go if you have to,' said Rochester-*san*. 'I never see those lights go on in Oxford Street without wanting to get out of London in a hurry. What is it you say: I go and I return?'

'*Itte mairimasu.*'

'Return, Akira.'

'I will. One day.'

'Chin chin,' Rochester-*san* gulped. 'Pity to waste this stuff. I'll see you down.' As he rose from his huge swivel chair, his new, or restored, authority was evident, but Suzuki was pleased to see that he had not lost a certain permanent boyishness, an air of receptivity that Suzuki had come to value in others, having begun to accept it within himself. It was the unfinished look. Rochester-*san*'s gaze, even as he took Suzuki's arm, had wandered beyond the window.

'He's probably working on a new thriller over there,' said Rochester-*san* abstractedly. 'I started one myself once. Perhaps I should look at it again.'

*

154

Lionel moved more of his stuff into Suzuki's room as Suzuki moved out. It was a neat transition. Lionel's path back to prosperity, he explained, would be through rented property, and in that field the Japanese tenant was a key factor.

'Ethel's the one who knows all about that, aintcher?' Lionel slapped her on the bottom.

'You Japs are the tenants to have,' she told Suzuki, kissing him fondly on the cheek. 'You were the only wild one, and look how easy *you* were. Mind how you go. Don't choke on a chop-stick.'

'You been an inspiration, Akira,' said Lionel over their last long hand-shake. 'I'll be working on your language just as hard as you done on ours.' Lionel added a carefully enunciated phrase of Japanese which, unless he actually meant to be starting a discussion about naval architecture in the Edo period, conveyed nothing except his good intentions.

'You will soon have it mastered,' said Suzuki. The big black Mercedes would have waited for ever, but it was time to go.

*

They stopped at the clinic on the way to the airport. The driver did not need directions. A Pakistani who insisted on being called by his first name, he had, he said, been driving for Sir Ernest since the earliest days.

'Your English is excellent,' said Suzuki.

'Well, in my country we speak it, of course.'

'Of course.'

'And then we spoke it again in Kenya.'

'Yes.'

'But you need a long time before you are beginning to get the hang of it. To cotton on, as they say.'

'Yes.'

*

Jane, though awake, was vague at first.

'Ron?'

'Suzuki. Akira. Sue.'

'Oh, hello. I've been sick.'

'I know. I'm sorry I couldn't be more help.'

'It wasn't your fault. I've always been funny. It goes back to when I was little. I couldn't keep anything together.'

'You have been very important to me.'

'Have I? Are you going home now?'

'Yes.'

'Will you be back?'

'Yes. And I'll be in touch.'

'Touch me now.'

'Like this?' He stroked her cheek, so clear he could see through it.

'You've got lovely hands, Sue. First thing I loved about you.'

'Was that in the bookshop?'

'No. When you thumped that bloke. I loved you after that. *Oo*, you were masterful.'

'I have to go.'

'I showed the article and the interview to a journalist friend of mine and they paid me for using some bits of it. Did it come out?'

'It was fine. But you must finish the next one by yourself.'

'I'm going to be a film director.'

'Are you? That's good.'

'Tired now.'

*

The Mercedes climbed onto the flyover leading to the M4 with such a surge of power that Suzuki felt it could have flown to Japan all by itself. The telephone rang.

'For you, I think,' said the driver. 'I will put up the partition.'

In vast privacy, a tumbler of Scotch in his hand, Suzuki listened to the unmistakably sensual voice of the girl with the unpronounceably mellifluous name.

'I hope you've poured yourself a drink.'

'Yes. I have. Where are you?'

'Klosters. Can you see a little box in there with the drinks? All wrapped up like a present, with a ribbon round it?'

'Yes.'

'Undo the ribbon.'

'I've undone it.'

'Unwrap the box.'

'I've unwrapped it.'

'Have you looked inside?'

'I'm looking.'

'Do you see the watch?'

'I can see it.'

'I thought you should have a nice thin one. That one you've got sticks up in the air a bit. Japanese are supposed to be subtle. Have you put it on?'

'I've put it on.'

'Do you like it?'

'It's perfect. Perfectly chosen. Everything around you is perfectly chosen.'

'Yes. And I chose you, too, didn't I? But you liked someone else better, didn't you?'

'Just differently. Will I see you again?'

'One day in Tokyo I'll come up and ask you the time.'

'I look forward to it.'

SEVENTEEN

A T HEATHROW, after queueing for a long time at one of
the JAL economy class check-in desks, Suzuki found that
he had been elevated to first class. He had never seen the inside
of a first-class lounge before and for a while he did not realise
the drinks were free. In the front cabin of the 747 the seats
were set alarmingly far apart, like thrones. On the first long
leg to Anchorage he chose Western food, on the assumption
that it would be the last he would see of it for some time. The
air-hostess changed costume to serve dinner. In kimono she
had the willowy grace of a Utamaro woodcut. Suzuki worked
his way through the *foie gras* and the *tournedos Rossini* and the
fruit tart and the *petits fours*. When the hostess saw how much
he liked the Krug she brought a silver bucket on a stand and
left a whole fresh bottle of it with him. Suzuki's head swam.
The North Pole was below him. Soon he would be halfway
home. Across the aisle an old man was sitting on his seat cross-
legged, eating a Japanese meal with flying chop-sticks and full
sound effects. Another old man cleared his sinus passages res-
onantly all the way through the movie. It was *A Room With A
View*. The beautiful Helena Bonham-Carter enunciated with

exemplary precision. Suzuki turned up the volume as far as it would go, trying to shut out the sound of the man snorting. There was a time when it would have been no bother.

At Anchorage Suzuki bought perfume, as Shimura-*san* had advised, the duty-free rate being better there than at Heathrow or Narita. He bought little bottles of Chanel No 5 for the women in his family and for the woman of his own he would meet one day; perhaps soon now; perhaps sooner than he would like. On the leg to Narita he ate Japanese food, although when the hostess brought another bottle of champagne he did not object. He was going home to a cold reception. Shimura-*san* would shake his head. But how much did that matter? Suzuki would have the flat in Ochanomizu with the living-room so big that you could walk around the table without moving any of the chairs. His novel would find a public of some kind. He already knew how it ended: the Japanese man and the English girl jumping hand in hand from the balcony to die impaled in the fountain full of light.

He would wear a roll-necked sweater under his suit instead of a collar and tie. He would sit all day in the coffee shop and be the leading young writer of a new school, lost between worlds, like space. He would cope with loneliness, having known it at first hand. It would be his territory.

He felt his head fill with blood. The plane was sinking southwards to meet his homeland drifting west. At Narita nobody asked him to open his briefcase. So Suzuki carried his future through the barrier and onto the bus, and the bus took him between the long fences into the colossal city which even through his headache he was suddenly eager to see again, with the fresh eye of the homecoming stranger.